THESE BATTERED HANDS

LAUREL ULEN CURTIS

These Battered Hands
Published by Laurel Ulen Curtis
© 2015, Laurel Ulen Curtis

Cover Design by Hang Le
Formatting by Champagne Formats

ISBN-13: 978-1517496012
ISBN-10: 1517496012

DEDICATION

To my B x 3 girls who would drop anything and
everything for me—
Thanks for proving to me that I've got it better
than anyone else.

xx

This story is an Adult Contemporary Romance taking place in the Summer of 2016.

PROLOGUE

His eyes were like actual pools of water—moving, flowing, and changing color along with depth. Each time his focus shifted, so did mine, zeroing in on a new fleck of deep blue and trying to help it float through the much more abundant aqua. Their magnetism made it hard to focus on his words, but I wouldn't have traded those moments spent studying their nuances for all of the words in the dictionary.

Sure, looks were shallow and words could mean everything, but in those split seconds when his eyes changed before my own, I would have sworn on my every Olympic medal it was the opposite.

And right now, I needed the comfort of that feeling. I needed it to swaddle me in its warmth and make everything feel right again.

The word wrong had never been a concept worthy of my focus, but as I tried to make sense of what was happening, denying its existence was no longer an option.

Up felt like down and left very nearly tricked me into believing it was right.

Voices called out to me constantly and on repeat, but none of them were the one I wanted. Like they were speaking through water, every pronunciation of my name seemed foreign and unwelcome, and my brain did nothing but scream another.

I tried valiantly to talk my uncooperative body into bending to my will, but for the first time in my life it *wouldn't*.

Digging deep down into my gut, I found the last vestiges of my energy and willed them into one single action.

Into one single word.

"Nik."

Priorities shifted and silence mocked me.

My entire life had been a series of events all specifically driven toward this very moment. I'd known all of my work was meant to culminate in a flourish of glory and significance. I'd known there'd be a second in time when I knew why each part of my life had played out the way it had. Why I'd worked, why I'd sweat, why I'd fought to keep going well after most people's journeys were done.

I'd *even* known it would probably happen now—on this stage, in front of all of these people.

I'd just had the timing wrong by about three minutes.

But I knew now.

This was it.

The thing I found myself wanting most during this moment— that was everything.

He was everything.

CHAPTER ONE

Callie

Ripping the last lingering piece of loose skin off of my palm and ignoring the accompanying sting, I threw it in the garbage and bent down to grab my Bars bag from its place against the wall. After three hours of hard work, the tape at the top of my left ankle was starting to curl into itself, pulling away from the pre-wrap and skin and fraying at the edges. I mindlessly studied the threads of its composition, sticking to the perimeter of the large room to avoid having to pay attention.

When you walked through an actively occupied gym, awareness was something you couldn't afford to be short on. Learning new skills and flipping your body through the air while practicing some new form of contortion (or torture) took enough concentration on its own. Therefore, we had a running rule that the person not actively involved in some form of gymnastics was the primary party accountable for safety. By sticking to the unused two foot board around the

3

outside, I abdicated myself of the tedious responsibility.

It wasn't that I didn't care, or that I didn't have the same goals as nearly every athlete in the building, but I had something that they didn't.

Time.

A fucking lot of it.

Having just turned twenty-six, I was now officially the oldest elite gymnast in the country. With two trips to the Olympics under my belt, I was headed for a third—and feeling every bit of my age.

Not only did my body deny me things it once agreed to with abandon, but the entire sport had taken on an air it never had.

Put simply, I was lonely.

One of the things I'd always loved about gymnastics is that I'd never felt alone. No task was independent, even when it very much *was*. Support came in bountiful supply and radiated from all directions. But in the last couple of years, for me, all that was once there had started to dwindle.

People resented a woman who couldn't be happy with two trips to the Olympics. Every spot was precious, *goddammit*. Why in the hell did I need to take one when I'd already lived the dream twice over?

Half of the time, I didn't even know the answer. But my drive never dwindled, and each time someone said I couldn't or shouldn't, I turned their naysaying into fuel for my fire.

Add that to the painfully obvious age gap—most of these girls were in their early teens—and it made for a complete cultural divide. What could we possibly have in common?

As it turned out, not much.

Their Justin Bieber giggles were the sounds of my nightmares, and, for me, gossiping about homework and boys lost its interest about ten years ago. They knew the pain of a hard week's worth of bumps and bruises and the sting of a bucket full of ice water.

But they didn't know what it felt like to be past the point of help, their bodies demanding real rest and care that no tape or Ace bandage could provide.

I didn't begrudge them their health, and I certainly didn't wish my aches or pains on anyone. But as the divide grew on the inside, the outside did a valiant job of trying to keep pace.

Unzipping my grip bag, I pulled out my grips and clutched them in one hand, freeing up my access to the wristbands below them.

The grips tucked easily under my arm as I pulled each band onto my wrists, settling them into the position I'd learned was just right. Not too high and not too low, the Goldilocks sweet spot was secure and comfortable at the same time.

At twenty-six, I'd spent so many hours with grips and lion paws (wrist supports) on my wrists, that the absence of them made me feel as naked as a stripper on her first night. Any touch of fresh air pebbled the unsuspecting skin.

But like this, with my wristbands on and my grips velcroed tight, everything felt right in my world. At least on the outside.

Sauntering up to the chalk bowl, I grabbed the wire brush and roughed up the already worn leather of each hand. A water bottle hung on the edge of the bowl, but people like me—well versed in practical experience—knew that I had my own personal moisture maker at my disposal that was a far better option.

Don't ask me the science behind it, but spit just worked better. Period. It wasn't sanitary or PC, but neither of those things were ever the kind of discouragement known for stopping me.

Pulling each hand up individually I spit into the palm of the left and then the right, going back for seconds when my first hand lacked the coverage I'd been seeking. I'd done it a million times, but as I dipped both hands into the bowl, the sound of a very *male*, very *deep* throat clearing alerted me that this would be a time like no other.

Startled, my eyes jumped from the chalk to him, and my spit-soaked hands stayed artfully pressed into the loose powder at the bottom of the bowl.

Vivacious, vivid blue eyes launched themselves toward me as if assisted by catapults and a knowing smirk settled into the corner of some of the plumpest lips I'd ever seen. They were perfect in a completely un-ridiculous, normal way, and the shock of his starkly black, overabundant hair made it nearly impossible to get lost in any feature other than those two.

I wanted to explore the rest of him, as you do on any first meeting, but he ruined it with words.

"Calia?"

"Yeah," I replied cautiously, fully registering that he was a stranger in my gym—my safe place—for the first time.

"Nikolai Bagrov," he said by way of introduction, shoving a hand out toward me to shake.

My eyes flicked quickly from him to my spit hands, still tucked safely in the harbor of the chalk bowl, and back again. It wasn't something I'd ever been conscious of before, but I'd never been propositioned for a handshake directly after either.

He followed my eyes a beat behind, realizing what had me balking quickly.

A low, sexy chuckle swept out his mouth and across his face, completely transforming his features from intimidatingly handsome to warmly welcoming in a heartbeat. I'd never been one for theatrics, but I'd be lying if I said there wasn't some small twinge deep in the valves of my heart that realized how disarming it was.

His hand never even threatened to retreat. "I'm not scared of a little spit. Shake my hand, Calia."

"Callie," I corrected as I reached for his hand, heedlessly minding his command. Normally, I went with the flow of my name, accepting it as it came and swallowing my insecurity at its formal version. But with him, I wanted to hear him call me Callie from the beginning.

"Callie," he repeated, shaking my hand with a nice, solid pump before taking his hand back and sliding it into the pocket of his perfectly fitted, blue athletic pants.

I immediately knew I'd made the right decision at the sound of my name on his lips, a delicate shiver making my spine sashay slightly from side to side.

Moments passed, and an awkward silence started to take shape. He seemed to be mulling something over in his head, but he wasn't saying anything and I had nothing to go on. And my own thoughts raced at too quickly a speed, making any attempt to latch on to one or all futile.

"Can I—" I started at the same time he blurted, "You can—"

Relieved to not be in charge, I gestured for him to continue and zipped my mouth.

He took one more deep breath, and then started over. "I'm a new coach here."

"Oh, cool," I shrugged, relaxing for the first time since he'd opened his mouth.

People cycled in and out occasionally, but aside from the occasional consult, I was largely in charge of myself and I liked it that way. My parents owning the gym not only helped in the way of funding such an expensive sporting endeavor, but it also gave me the freedom to train how and when I wanted.

"No," he replied, confusing me by answering my non-question with what I thought was a completely unrelated answer. He shook his head, looking a little nervous. "I'm *your* new coach."

"What? Says who?"

"Your—"

"My father," I finished for him, knowing the answer as soon as I asked the question. If one of my parents was going to meddle, I could pretty much guarantee it would be the one with the Y chromosome.

To him, his dreams were my own and vice versa. In my world,

the one where the gym was my country, and my father was the government, freedom wasn't really quite free. He had veto power and he used it, but only when he thought it was *in my best interest.*

And I wasn't the one who decided when that was.

Nikolai shrugged, managing to look both bashful and unrepentant at once.

I turned away, headed back to the chalk bowl, and started my process all over again, talking through my back as I went. "Listen, Nikolai—"

"Just call me Nik."

I rolled my eyes knowing he couldn't see it. "Listen, *Nik*, I've been coaching myself for the last four years, aside from my time on the actual *Olympic* team. I think I've got it handled."

I gasped as his face appeared right in front of mine, his body stooped low with his white t-shirt-covered shoulders curling in toward the front while his eyes worked at pinning my jumpy ones down with a spear-like intensity.

"All due respect, *Callie*, but if you weren't lacking something, you would have been satisfied two Olympics ago."

My eye started to twitch way in the back, where the muscles attach to the socket, the way it always did when someone hit a particularly sensitive nerve. He wasn't saying anything I didn't know or hadn't realized, but the fact that he thought he had me all figured out when the complexities of my psyche were still a twisted mess *to me* really irked me.

At one point, I'd been so lost inside of my own inner workings, gridlocked by the traffic noise of my insecurities and an equally powerful stubbornness to "hard-work" my way out of them, my mom had suggested I see a therapist.

I hadn't done it, obviously; bullheadedness had always been my more dominant emotion.

After rejecting someone's psychoanalysis who literally studied, practiced, and got paid to do it, I wasn't about to let some stranger step into my life one minute and mindfuck me the next.

My mind wasn't nearly that loose or easy—even for criminally attractive men with uniquely layered, multifaceted, *dangerous-as-fuck* blue eyes.

What an—

CHAPTER TWO

Nik

Asshole.

Opinions are like them in that everybody's got one.

In Callie's case, as a world-class athlete, there was no question in my mind that people fed them to her like potato chips, unable to stick to just one. The salt would no doubt eventually numb her to the taste and the sensation, and I had a feeling she didn't particularly like Sour Cream and Opinion fucking chips anymore.

But I had a feeling my vision of her wasn't far off. She was missing something, and even she *knew* it.

I could see it in her eyes, the way they narrowed and twitched. Her face bled emotion despite her efforts to disguise it, and in my experience, no one ever got that annoyed unless faced with the unwelcome truth.

"Look. I realize we don't actually know one another—"

"*At all*," she interrupted with a dirty raise of her dark eyebrow.

Carrying on as though she hadn't spoken, I expanded on my point. "But when it comes to gymnastics, it's my job to make assumptions about you."

I had to judge her as an actual competition judge would, not as though I knew her or the reasons behind her actions, but as though her actions alone spoke for themselves. It was a sport of snap judgements really, deciding in an instant if a toe was pointed enough or if a leg had a slight bend.

"We're going to become close over the next eight weeks before training camp, and you're going to learn to trust me and my opinions."

We had to. She had to learn to trust me, and I had to do the things to earn it. If not, I didn't know where I'd be. And she'd be exactly where she was now, searching for some unknown something.

"You sound pretty sure of yourself," she accused.

"No. I'm not sure of myself," I corrected. "Not like you're thinking. I *am* certain of your determination though. That kind of fight, that kind of grit that goes into the amount of work you've put in … "

She was attempting to win a bid to her third Olympics for God's sake. There was no doubt the woman knew how to work.

"There's no way you'll let it all go to waste just to spite some asshole coach."

She considered my words carefully, her eyes jumping around the room as if searching for a physical loophole. Cognizant of the precarious state of her opinion of me, I had to fight to keep my bubbling laughter from boiling over.

Eventually, inevitability won out and her pinball eyes transitioned into a much more subdued glare.

I watched her settle into the anger, accept it, and fuel herself and an equally strong emotional wall with its power. She didn't want me close, she didn't want me thinking I could get that way, and anger was a good way to reinforce her point.

But I honestly didn't mind. That kind of fire and drive was what made her an elite level athlete, and there's no way she would have been at this point in her life, needing somebody like me to step in, if she hadn't harnessed it successfully.

I wouldn't have let some random fucknut come in and tell me what to do on day one either.

Her ponytail swung violently over her slender shoulder as she turned and callously ripped the freshly stuck together velcro of her grips apart. Each ridge of her starkly cut muscles shimmied and danced with the movement, trailing into the darkness of cover provided by her purple, crushed velvet leotard.

Her face was hidden but her hunched shoulders expressed every vivid detail of her emotion as though they were wired directly to it. I didn't bother to hide my smile knowing she wouldn't see it, but I did manage to stop myself from pointing out that she had yet to complete even one skill on Bars before leaving. I knew she wouldn't want to hear it, and I knew she needed to release some steam out of the valve of my unintentional pressure cooker.

What I *didn't* know was *her*. What made her tick and smile and what I could do to enhance it. And something in me burned to change that.

I didn't know what it was. If I felt like I had something in common or if the buttons in her personality just felt instinctually like they lined up with the holes of mine.

It was human nature to wonder and ponder and work at sorting it out. But you couldn't find the answer when you didn't even know the exact question.

"What's with the pariah status you have going?" I asked as she walked in front of me, changing the subject and looking everywhere but at her in order to keep my thoughts professional.

Her body was spectacular—something I wasn't surprised by given she spent thirty plus hours a week in the gym completing rigorous physical activity—but something else about the way she carried herself had my eyes itching to take a closer look. At the line of her back. The curve of her hip as it settled into her perfectly tight ass. The rock-solid definition of her thighs.

Okay. So maybe I'd looked a little.

"What?" she asked, whipping her ten inch long, glossy ponytail over her muscular shoulder once more. It was obviously a signature move. At least around me.

When her chocolate eyes met mine they sparkled with something unmistakable.

Dislike. *Strong* dislike.

With thirty hours a week of togetherness ahead of us, I'd have to work on that.

"I thought Olympic medals made you into more of a celebrity than the vibe I'm getting here," I explained, completely ignoring the stank eye and focusing instead on the lush lashes around it.

Two Team Silvers and an individual Bronze on the Beam, Callie was accomplished. I'd gotten lost in watching old YouTube videos of her, the memories of watching her when the games had aired on TV coming back as I did.

Her name might not be commonplace the world over, but anyone with any association to the sport of gymnastics knew it well.

But here in her world, she was like a solar eclipse. No one looked directly at her as we made our way across the gym. I didn't know if it was for fear that it would burn out their retinas or something else.

She laughed, half with humor and half without it. There was acceptance in her voice, but it didn't completely mask the bitterness and burn.

"They fan-girled between Olympics one and two. Once they knew I was hoping for a third, my appeal kind of died out. Turned into much more of a resentment cocktail."

"Really?"

That surprised me.

She pretended to shrug it off. "I was never much of a mentor anyway."

Self-deprecation mixed with longing.

I'd never heard the exact combination before now. It sounded eerily calm but undeniably scratchy. Like it got caught in the back of her throat as she forced herself to spit it out.

Her body turned to shut me out, her part in the conversation done.

Instead of pushing what was clearly an uncomfortable subject, I moved on.

"Where are we headed?"

"Floor," she answered shortly without turning around.

I nodded my head from behind her but held my silence.

Eventually, it got to her.

Another thing I'd have to remember for future reference because part of my job was to get under her skin.

Irritation instigates emotion, and emotion opens the door for change. Not at first—first comes anger. But anger eventually bleeds into reflection, and reflection breeds acceptance. And acceptance—*that's* what leads to change.

"What?" she asked, turning to meet my eyes.

I shook my head with a smile, completely belying my innocence. "I didn't say anything."

"I could hear you thinking," she argued with a frown.

My smile deepened and my arms crossed easily across my chest in silent challenge.

"You could *hear* me thinking?"

Her face wrinkled slightly with contempt. "Don't mock me. I know you know what I mean."

"You know I know what you mean?"

"Stop repeating everything I say!" she snapped, throwing her grips bag to the ground and cinching her ponytail tighter before slamming both angry hands to her trim hips.

"Sorry," I fake-apologized, leaning slightly toward her as I spoke for emphasis. "I was just making sure you understood *what* you were saying."

The gap between her eyebrows narrowed meaningfully.

Settling my hands into my pockets, I felt my smile reach all the way up to my eyes. "Looks like you think we know each other just *a little bit* after all."

"Great," she mumbled to herself, turning back in the direction of the floor, jerking her bag back off of the ground, and talking as she walked. "An observant smart ass for a coach. Just what I've always wanted."

"Better than a clueless dumb ass, no?" I called to her back as she dropped her grip bag at the side of the floor mat and walked to the far corner. Other coaches and gymnasts looked on with curious eyes, prompted by the volume of my voice, but I ignored them, focusing solely on the slight curvature taking shape at the corner of her mouth.

That tiny change in shape, that small token of humor gave me hope. I'd have her liking me before long.

Surprised at the intensity of the feeling, I jumped when the warmth grew in my chest at the prospect. I hadn't thought I would care if she liked me, one way or another, as long as she got the training she needed and I kept my job as her coach. But only one conversation in, I found myself wanting it a lot.

And I wasn't quite sure why.

Waiting her turn in a line of much younger gymnasts, she watched as they took turns tumbling in a cross pattern. It was one in a long list of rarely spoken rules in the world of gymnastics. Put into practice informally at every gym across the country and national competitions alike, each corner took a turn tumbling diagonally from one corner to another. Staggering back and forth from opposite corners gave ample time for a gymnast to clear their corner after completion of their pass with little to no downtime.

Glancing occasionally at the sloppy form of a newly seasoned, almost unbearably young Level Eight gymnast on their full twisting layout, I focused primarily on Callie and the way she watched and waited.

Gymnastics was largely a young person's sport, and it was that way for a couple of reasons. Not only did the unmarred minds of the youth recognize and react less to innate fear, they also vibrated with unconfined energy. Their bodies drove their young minds to complete each task.

Conversely, Callie's practiced mind *forced* her largely uncooperative body.

Leg extended and toe pointed with precision, it reached out in front of her tapping the ground in preparation before her pass.

Her steps were that of ease, but the power of her thighs did undeniable work as she lunged into her round off, whipped through her back-handspring, and set high and tight with her elbows by her ears for an easy and over exaggerated layout.

She was fun to watch, but I could tell she moved in half measures.

I called her over with a flick of a finger, smiling at the answering roll of her eyes. I'd never gotten quite so much enjoyment out of annoying someone before. In fact, I usually bowed down to the unbearable urge to people please.

I couldn't figure out how this could be so different and yet feel so good.

"What?" she asked when she arrived. Her tone wasn't one of excitement or avidity for learning. It was one of annoyance.

I felt a flutter in my gut.

Obviously something was wrong with me. Maybe the Chinese

food I'd had for lunch was bad.

I shook my head internally, carefully constructing the points of my advice to make sure it came out simple and organized and easy to follow.

"You're not harnessing the power from one skill to use in another. You need to drive through your toes more, use the energy from your back-handspring to drive you up, rather than wasting it all through your flat feet into the ground."

She shrugged her shoulder, waved me off.

"It was a warm-up pass."

She turned to leave, but I wasn't done, so I interrupted the movement with a gentle touch of my hand to her smooth shoulder.

Her eyes jumped to mine as though zapped by the contact, and a corresponding tingle ran all the way from my fingertips to the depths of my stomach.

I had to mentally coerce my eyes back to normal size and fight for concentration—forcibly remove my hand from her shoulder.

"It doesn't work like that. Each pass you make forms a habit, and the amount of passes only grows over time. You've got a lot of both."

She looked even more miffed, and at first I didn't understand.

Then, I did. And I was the one rolling my eyes.

"I'm not saying you're old. Jesus. I'm saying you're experienced."

"Experience is a *good* thing."

"It is," I agreed, which seemed to satisfy her. For about a second. "It can also work against you."

"How's that?" she demanded.

"Not all habits are good ones. In fact, a big fucking heap of them are the exact opposite—"

"Get to the point," she interrupted.

Foregoing any further explanation and succumbing to the fact that she wasn't going to let me cushion anything with pleasantries, I gave it to her straight. "You're talented, but you're completely wasting it." She started to protest, so I threw up a hand. "Stop being lazy and put some power through your goddamn feet!"

Indignation fired her veins and reddened the brown of her irises. "You watch one pass and you think you have the right to call me lazy?" she nearly shrieked.

Heads turned in our direction. We both ignored them.

"You're not lazy. Your tumbling is." She drew in a quick, fury-filled breath, no doubt gearing up to let me have it. I didn't give her the chance. "And I've watched you more than one time. I've been watching you since you were a seventeen year old kid competing in your first World's. Your feet have been lazy the entire damn time."

"You know what? I think I'm done for today," she fumed quietly, grabbing her bag from the ground behind her and sparing only one look to the now-gawking crowd as she stormed away.

Unwilling to let a little public confrontation end our first day on a sour note, I followed her, only managing to catch up at the entrance to the locker room.

"Callie! Wait!" I grabbed her shoulder to turn her again, but this time, there was no zap—only a shake to knock it loose.

"I said I'm done for today." Her face was serious and unrelenting. End of discussion.

I softened my voice and my eyes and tried to understand why she was so averse to advice. Granted, I hadn't exactly executed the smoothest of deliveries, but when it came to tumbling I knew what I was talking about.

"I'm just trying to help."

Her face broke slightly, but the words she spoke next didn't have so much as a crack.

"You said it yourself. I've been doing this my entire life—at this level since I was a *seventeen year old kid*." Locking her body tight, I watched as she forced the words to clear her throat. "Where were you?" She paused for the briefest of beats and then answered her

18

own question. "*Watching me.* Maybe I'm not the lazy one after all."

Then she was gone. Around the corner and into the locker room, safely ensconced in a place where I couldn't follow her.

I wanted to. But I couldn't.

Nearly numb from the unexpected encounter, I turned on my heel and stalked across the gym toward the office. Her father, Frank, had requested a meeting after I finished with Callie for the day. An assessment of sorts to see if I was really going to work out.

He had a personal hand in Callie, and despite what I'd told her, the decision to keep me as her coach wasn't exactly final.

Today was meant to be a trial of sorts.

I ignored the stares of the other coaches, and instead focused on using deep breaths to calm me down.

I couldn't explain the rapid beat of my heart or the intensity with which I felt her comments. The difference in what she saw me as and what I was niggled at me, itching the voice box in my throat and tempting me to go back and have it out with her. We both reacted too strongly for having just met each other, and as much as I couldn't fathom an argument feeling welcome, with her it had. Because I could feel the way she felt mirrored in myself. Defensive and apprehensive and passionate all at once. So many emotions all swirled together canceled each other out. All that was left was confusion.

Still, I didn't need to be worked up when I went into his office, so I took the confusion as a godsend and embraced it. Because I didn't have enough time to dissect all of my complicated feelings either.

All I knew was that I should have been mad. If someone else had spoken to me the way she had, insinuated the things she had, I would have been furious.

But I wasn't angry. Not at all.

I was just *interested.*

I knocked on the office door, and it opened immediately. A smirk lined the cheek of Frank's face, and it took seeing it for me to realize that his office had a window that looked over the gym. He'd no doubt had a front row seat to our display.

Though, I wouldn't have exactly expected his reaction to be a smile.

He gestured to the chair in front of his desk, so I sat, crossing one foot over the other leg.

"So you met Calia?" he started nonchalantly, grabbing a bottle of water off of his desk and taking a swig.

"Yes, sir." Obviously.

"She give you a hard time?"

The way he smiled put me on edge, and I wasn't sure why.

It wasn't that she hadn't given me a hard time. She most definitely had.

I was pretty sure he'd witnessed it just like everybody else in the gym.

But her emotion had been honest and real and completely uncontrived.

Something about the way his tone resonated felt belittling of that emotion. Almost how I imagined you'd view a child throwing a tantrum.

But Callie wasn't a child, and that judgement of her felt unfair on a basic level. It didn't take into account the muddy waters that churned inside her beautiful skin. Everything I knew said it' was impossible to keep from being rough on the outside when you're ragged underneath.

And Callie was. I didn't know what drove each impulse, but I knew she had some kind of deep-seated issue. Whether it was an actual catalyst or self-sustained demons, she was fighting something. Something I guessed she'd been fighting a while.

I measured my words carefully. "She was ... resistant."

"Ha!" he barked through a laugh. "Resistant." He shook his head. "I usually call it stubborn. Like hell resisting an ice storm."

I fought the urge to cringe, smoothing the edges of my mouth carefully. His bark held no bite or malice, but for some reason I was being overly sensitive about a woman I'd just met. He'd known her for her entire life. The rationalist in me knew I had to defer to his knowledge on this one, so with one deep breath, I forced myself to let the indignation go.

I cleared my throat slightly and shifted my right ankle further across my left knee.

"If you don't mind my asking …" He raised his brows. "Why me?" His chin jerked back slightly.

This wasn't the kind of question people normally asked. Something about looking directly into the mouth of a gift horse.

"There are a ton of other coaching options out there for someone as talented as Callie."

He smiled more deeply at my use of her nickname. Like he got the answer to some sort of question he'd been waiting patiently to ask—without actually asking it.

"You could have past Olympic team coaches here, and instead you've got a power tumbler like me."

He leaned casually into the edge of his desk and crossed his feet at the ankles. The look on his face made me want to stop talking, but this far into my speech, I had no choice but to continue.

"No offense, but I don't get it."

He pursed his lips and grabbed his chin, but there was no contemplation. He already knew exactly what he was going to say.

"Let me ask you a question, Nik."

Okay.

"How many people do you think there are in this gym who call her Callie?"

Of all the things I thought he would ask, that wasn't one of them.

Women's gymnastics experience, recommendations from other people—those were the things I thought he'd want to know.

21

Struggling to calculate based on a rough number of pupils I thought attended, I started to lob out a random number.

"Uh—"

He chuckled, and then saved me from my ignorance. "Three."

"Three?" I questioned.

"You, her mother, and me."

I didn't understand.

A shrug hefted the weight of his shoulders up around his ears. "Call it a hunch, but I think she'll relate to you better than some old fogey of a coach with no concept of a young adult's reality."

I didn't hide my recoil thinking about the way we related today.

He just laughed.

"It's like I can see the thoughts as they run through your mind."

Hopefully, that was a limited time thing. I didn't need him reading my thoughts when I was picturing naked women.

Or thinking about picturing naked women.

Shit.

"Your interaction today was passionate, sure, but you're one up on everyone else."

"Sir?"

"You interacted. Period." He shrugged. "She ignores everyone else."

"We caused a little bit of a scene."

He chuckled again. "All the people watching you?"

I nodded.

"They were probably startled to hear her voice, she hasn't spoken to anyone in so long." Excitement clashed with the context of his next words. "Hell, she yelled at you!"

"I noticed, sir."

He winked, and it put my earlier ill-feelings at ease. At least about him.

Today as a whole felt like a foreign, jumbled-up mess. Everything I'd learned about myself in the last twenty-eight years was being overruled and replaced by a newer, completely opposing emotion.

At least, that's what it felt like right now.

God. I needed to clear my head. Start over. Recalibrate or something.

"Keep up whatever you're doing. It may not feel right now, but it will in the end."

The weird thing was, it *did* feel right. Natural. It felt like we'd been ribbing each other for years.

"She may not ever like you—"

Well, that was inspiring.

"But I have a feeling she will learn to listen. And that's what's important," he stated resolutely.

Was it?

I wasn't so sure.

Instead of commenting directly, I shook it off and asked about the one thing I knew would help me the most.

"Is it still alright if I tumble here after hours?"

"Of course." He reached behind him, leaned over the desk, and pulled open one of the drawers. With a bang, he slid it shut and reached to pass me something. "Here's a key. Just lock up when you're done."

"Thank you."

He nodded. "You shouldn't have to wait long. Everyone should be clearing out pretty soon."

His grip was strong as I shook his hand and stood to leave. When he smiled genuinely again, I started to feel silly. I was compelled to understand everything in every new situation immediately by an innate desire to be liked and do well, but in this case, it wasn't doing anything but cocking the gun aimed straight at my own foot.

I didn't need to know every detail about Callie or her father right now. I just needed to settle in and be myself. I had a penchant for hard work, and this effort would be no different. The rest would work itself out in time.

When I stepped outside and the door closed behind me, I unintentionally surveyed the room and the people in it.

Two thorough scans later, I didn't find what I was looking for.

She'd said she was leaving, and I'd been in her father's office for enough time for her to do it unnoticed. I guess a part of me just expected I'd get to have another word with her. Something less toxic. Less heated. Less judgmental—on both ends.

One of the coaches I'd met earlier—Jim, I think—waved goodbye with a smirk on his face.

"See you tomorrow," I called out in reply. He just shook his head in the affirmative.

Done being watched, I headed for the exit instead of hanging around. My bag was in my bike anyway, and I wanted to be able to change before I left tonight.

The new metallic charcoal paint of my Street Glide sparkled under the parking lot lights as soon as I opened the door. Crickets chirped in the field across the street, and the glow of the nearly full moon cast a shadow on the windshields of all of the remaining cars. Approaching ten PM, a slight sheen of dew had settled on every surface and pebbled tiny drops of water on the leather of my seat.

I'd always been a bike guy, and it had never been much of a weather issue this far south in Georgia. At least not where temperature was concerned. But now that I had a steady schedule and responsibility, I figured I'd need to look into a form of backup transportation when the rain got to be too much.

I lifted the saddlebag open and pulled out my bag, setting it on the seat so that I could focus on the bottom.

I kept a picture of my parents there, young and in love and fresh off the boat from Russia. My father was a dancer and my mother a gymnast. They worked incredibly hard from the moment they got here until the moment they died in a car accident six months ago. Tragic as it was for me, I always took solace in the fact that they went together—for them. A shining example of what made a good team, my father often pushed and pushed until my mother pulled and bent him to her will. He went willingly because it made sense. *They were both trying to go the same direction.*

There was nothing my father would have wanted more than to follow her to Heaven.

Expelling one shuddering breath, I shoved one hand through my overly shaggy hair and pulled the top of the saddlebag closed with the other.

Grabbing my bag, I headed back for the door and scooted into the bathroom while the remaining stragglers were making their way out.

I changed into shorts and wrapped both ankles, being sure to tape them comfortably tight. I also pulled out my thinner tape and attached my pinky finger—that I somehow managed to break all the time—to my ring finger as a preventive measure, and slipped one of those elastic headbands into my hair to keep it out of my face. Exiting the bathroom, I moved slowly, poking my head out first and finding the lights dimmed to appropriate "we're closed" levels.

The door only squeaked a little as I let it swing shut behind me, and pulled the switch closest to me back into the on position. The light made a hum, but it was the kind of sound that faded almost immediately because I was so conditioned to its background noise.

I chucked my bag to the side, a dull thud resonating as it hit the floor, pulled my t-shirt over my head and pitched it on top, and sank to my butt on the end of the long Rod floor to do a thorough stretch before I made any passes.

Quiet. Peaceful. Homey.

This was my favorite way to be in the gym—

CHAPTER THREE

Callie

Alone.

Such an ironic concept for me. I constantly felt it, but I never actually was.

Not until this time of night anyway. It was my favorite time to be here, and usually I didn't do anything. Just hung out on a mat somewhere and stared at the warehouse ceiling.

But I'd spent an extraordinary amount of time in the locker room tonight. Thinking. Fuming. Considering. And talking myself in circles.

I watched discreetly as girls came and went, grabbing their bags and heading back to a late night of hearty home-cooked food and homework. The late nights were relentless in the life of a gymnast, but so were the early mornings. I couldn't for the life of me remember a day that I'd slept past six or fallen asleep before midnight. Not one. In twenty-six years.

And I didn't see it changing.

Pulling my lavender, terry cloth pants out of my bag, I didn't bother to clean the chalk from my legs before pulling them on. I shut my locker quietly, but the sound of pounding on the rod floor made me jump.

I thought everyone was gone, and my parents normally locked me in on their way out. Creeping around the bench in the middle of the narrow room, I peeked out the door and sank down into a squat so I could see under the beams.

A tan, muscular back stood out against the bright blue waistband of his shorts, and his ankles faded into one big, white blob thanks to the tape. His right hand twitched minutely, the fingers curling into his palm softly, and he bounced on his toes just once before taking two long strides into his hurdle. His round off just barely skimmed the floor, the rods rippling with the force of his whip backs, and he ended with one of the highest, most explosive full-twisting layouts I'd ever witnessed.

It wasn't a simple pass for the layperson, but he certainly made it look that way.

My earlier words haunted me as though they were an actual ghost.

Maybe you're the lazy one.

Good one, Callie.

Walking with his head down, he followed the white line down the center of the thin strip of floor on his way back down to the beginning, and the ends of his too long hair flopped forward from the binding of a pretty girly headband.

Nik needed a haircut like I needed an attitude adjustment, but his abs did more than make up for it. Perfectly defined and well-honed with the muscle of a seasoned athlete, I couldn't take my eyes off of them. They weren't the kind of muscle a guy got from being in a gym and lifting weights.

They were the kind that actually helped lift stuff.

For him, that meant his body.

For me, it meant I was an even bigger fool for hitting him with the old "those who can't do, teach" jab.

As quietly as I could, I crept out the door and behind the beams, across the mat in the pit, and settled into the corner created by a standing mat and the wall just next to the bars. It afforded me the perfect view without disclosing my location to him. He didn't seem to know I was there, and I had no intention of changing that.

I just wanted to watch. To have my moment and let him have his, but spy on him all the same. I wanted to see someone else do the work for my enjoyment, and I wanted to do it in peace. And my hormones didn't mind the view either.

Disappointment flooded my veins fast and furiously as he stepped off the end of the rod floor and walked over to his bag.

He couldn't be done, could he?

He'd made two passes for shit's sake.

That's more than you did tonight, an evil (read: obnoxiously right) voice chided inside my head.

But, no. Two seconds later the evidence of his intent to continue rang out from his hands.

A slow beat filled the otherwise silent air, and then scratched to a halt as he changed the song. His head bent forward, and that went on a couple of times until he found the one he wanted, gently lobbed his phone on top of his bag, and turned back to the floor.

Panicked, I slid back into my hole and closed my eyes, like that could somehow prevent him from seeing me, and held my breath until I heard the telltale sounds of his feet starting his pass mixed with the harsh melody of a fast and furious Metallica song.

Just the frenzy of the music had my heart ready to beat out of my chest, and I wasn't even doing anything. I had no idea how he managed to tumble to it. Too scared to look soon enough, I missed that pass and had to wait for him to walk all the way back to this end to start a new one.

He took a couple of deep breaths, bounced on his toes again, and then he was gone. Round off, back-handspring, whip back, whip back, whip back, motherfucking full-twisting double goddamn layout. His power nearly shook the foundation of the goddamn warehouse, he drove through his toes so well, and once again I felt the fool for thinking I knew better about my stupid tumbling than he did.

At the exhale of my breath his head jerked in my direction, and I whipped my head around again, sinking into the mat and biting painfully into my cringing bottom lip.

Please don't let him see me, please don't let him see me.

The sound of the floor exploding let me know he hadn't as he started another pass and my head whipped out immediately, as not to miss the rest of the skills.

This time he finished with a double full-twisting double layout. And still made it look freaking easy.

No sweat shone on his forehead, and his hands didn't shake with unease. He was completely in his element, focused on the music and the skills and not in the slightest bit winded. He was practiced. He did this a lot, and he did it well.

I found myself hoping he'd stay all night as I watched pass after pass, each one increasing in difficulty and speed. Each skill had to be timed perfectly, each hand and foot placed with precision. And God, he was fun to watch.

He barely smiled, but I could see a glow light him up from within. He loved doing this. He loved it without bias or question, and he did it wholeheartedly.

In that moment, he didn't want to be doing anything but this, anywhere but here.

I used to know how that felt, and I longed to feel that way again.

After the fifteenth pass, I sank my butt to the floor and my back into the wall. I was tired from watching and he'd finally formed a few droplets of sweat on the center of his chest.

I couldn't actually *see* the droplets at this distance, but based on the glow, I could imagine.

By God, I could imagine.

The music still raged in the background and his stupid hair still flopped around his ears. But something else had changed in the time it took for me to watch those passes.

A part of me had accepted him as someone I could trust. Someone who I could relate to. Someone who just might end up knowing how I felt. I could see myself in him, at least the way I used to be. The way he worked at his own pace with no shortage of self-instilled ethic. I could see the years he'd put in to get to that point, plain as day in the level of his talent, and I knew it had to be equal to if not more than my own.

But all of those realizations cloaked more unknowns, the hows and whys of a talented athlete like him coaching me a real-life mystery.

He looked happy on the outside, but I knew better than anyone that no disguise should make you assume what's underneath. Funny people can be depressed. Outgoing girls can suffer from crippling self-esteem issues. And someone who seems sullen and withdrawn might just be happier in their head.

This pass would be tough, the increase in difficulty, as he progressed, speaking for itself. But he treated them all the same. The same little bounce of his toes, the same soft flex of his fingers.

Two bounding steps preceded a round off, back-handspring, double layout, whip back, whip back, and the grand finale—a triple pike.

Hysteria made me pull at the top of my leotard violently.

Was it hot in here?

What kind of twilight zone was this?

And how much energy did he have? I needed him to be done already.

Oh shit. Don't think about sex.

I said don't.

Don't.

DO NOT.

Stamina. Power. Flashes of his sweat-beaded skin slick against mine.

Too late.

If I knew what it felt like to orgasm, I'd imagine watching him do something like that felt similar. As a shiver worked its way down my spine and the muscles of his strong stomach flexed and contracted, I decided for possibly the first time ever, I'd be open to being proven wrong though.

Oh man. This was *not* the direction my thoughts needed to go about my coach.

I was just stressed and tired. That's all. This wouldn't become a regular thing. Nope. Definitely not.

Get me out of here.

Finally, he headed for his bag, switching off the stream of music and tossing his t-shirt over his shoulder. He rifled through the bag slowly, taking his goddamn time, and each passing second made my skin itch more and more to the point of crawling.

Standing to full height, he pulled the bag to his shoulder, rounded the corner.

A deep breath filled my lungs with fresh oxygen and released the tightening on my starved brain almost instantly.

Thank God.

I waited for him to be gone, the bang of the bathroom door signaling my movement like the bat signal did for Batman.

Mats compressed slightly under my tennis-shoe-encased feet as

I hauled ass back to the locker room door, grabbed my bag, and shot toward the door of the gym like it was on fire. I had only a short window of time to get out, and I planned to make the most of it.

The late night humidity nearly choked me as I transitioned into it at full speed, taking big gulps of the freedom it represented.

Unfortunately, I had only taken two steps in the direction of my car before the light slammed off behind me.

He was coming.

Honestly, it probably wouldn't have been that big of a deal if he'd seen me, but my mind was too far gone to accept it. The car and the far corner of the building were just about equidistant from me, and I of course, made the predictably bad, slasher film-esque decision to flee mindlessly for the cover of the building.

The door opened just as I rounded the corner, and my heart beat rapidly against the metal siding exterior.

Two silent bangs of my forehead later, I peeked around the corner to get a glance.

Well-fitted jeans encased his muscular legs, and his plain white t-shirt had returned to its flesh-covering duty.

He glanced at my car once before approaching a motorcycle that was parked even closer to me, but he didn't look my way. I didn't trust that the subterfuge would last.

Talk about royally screwing this up.

I had the nearly skin-evacuation-inducing urge to get out of there before he spotted me, but as I watched my car from the corner of the building with him in between, I realized one important thing.

I had nowhere to—

CHAPTER FOUR

Nik

Go.

As much as I doubted Callie would want to, my heart wouldn't stop shoving letters into the suggestion box of my brain.

"Ask," my heart said. "What does it hurt to ask?"

My heart sounded a little like a girl.

I shook my head at myself, squeezing my eyes shut to quiet the riotous fluctuation of my emotions.

I'd known she was there between my fourth and fifth tumbling passes. A shadow had lurked on the far wall of the warehouse from behind a stack of mats. The swish of a ponytail confirmed the shadow's identity.

She didn't know I knew she was there though, and that was where asking got tricky.

To me, I'd felt like she was sitting there next to me the whole time despite her efforts to stay hidden, and to my complete shock—I didn't mind.

I'd always liked to have my alone time at the end of the night. Always.

But tonight, with her, I'd liked having her there with me.

I was too confused to know what that meant, but I wasn't too confused to know I shouldn't be feeling it. Because I wasn't feeling strictly professional thoughts and affection a coach has for an athlete. Hell, there'd been no time to form that kind of a formal bond.

Instead, I was feeling a draw to a near stranger, the things I knew about her inciting feelings inside of me on a chemical level. Nerves buzzed with extra excitement and the good kind of anxiety churned in my gut.

Her unique sense of self, so skewed from what the rest of the world thought, the small glimpse I'd gotten of her personality, and the way she held back in a manner that only she could understand or explain—all of it made the "couldn'ts" seem like "shouldn'ts" and really only "maybe shouldn'ts" at that.

It'd all gone wrong from the start, the spit that sealed our first handshake seeming to swear me into an alternate universe.

What was right got twisted upside down, and nothing mattered more than finding the missing pieces of her puzzle.

"Do you want to go somewhere with me?" I called out into the silent darkness before I thought better of it.

And before I realized exactly how it sounded.

"Not for sex," I clarified loudly, and then rammed my face straight into my palm.

Really, Nik?

Smooth.

It only took five seconds to hear irritated shuffling, a few muttered curses, and an aggrieved but clear, "How'd you know I was here?"

She still wasn't visible, hidden by the corner of the building.

Not wanting to make the whole scenario any more embarrassing than it already was—for either of us—I decided to lie.

"Your car."

A couple additional seconds of quiet consideration passed.

"How'd you know it was *my* car?"

I cleared my throat and called out loudly once more. "I think it was the 'third Olympics or die' sticker in the back window."

"WHAT?" she shrieked, charging around the corner in horrified displeasure.

Angry, confused steps ate up the distance between us.

Of course, when she got there, there was no decal—never had been, thank God.

"Oh." A deep sigh. "You think you're being cute."

I smiled deeper into my cheeks, but verbally ignored the comment.

When the silence became too much, she scrambled to cover herself.

"I, um, fell asleep in the locker room." She cleared her throat once, twice, and ended with a third time. "What are *you* doing here?"

Her arms crossed over her chest as though to keep out a chill, but the hot air of a southern summer night sat stagnant around us. Any discomfort had to be coming from her encounter with me.

I wish I could have told her all her bumbling effort to make excuses was for her benefit alone. I didn't mind that she'd watched.

But my father always told me to think of a man's logic and completely reverse it. That's where I would find the answers for dealing with a woman.

I thought it was sound advice. My mother had smacked him.

A confirmation.

"Tumbling," I muttered instead, keeping it as simple as possible to avoid getting caught in a knot of unintended words.

She forced her eyes to widen and her jaw to relax like she didn't understand.

"Your dad gave me permission to train after hours. I'm a power tumbler," I explained simply, cringing slightly on the implication that I still intended to compete. I didn't.

I only did it for fun and to clear my head. I wasn't sure how I'd find mental peace when my body grew old and my joints broke down, but for now, it was my solace.

Her cheeks pinked just slightly with the embarrassment of her dishonesty and her hands rubbed roughly at her arms. She really thought I didn't know she'd watched me.

I let her have it. For now.

"So … I asked if you want to go somewhere with me."

Her feet drew her attention as her weight shifted back and forth between them. Nervous fingers twined and twisted with each other, whitening the skin with simple pressure. Her eyes jumped to mine, and her question was misleadingly simple. I thought I had her.

"Where?"

"Ah, see, I can't tell you that." I wagged my brows, leaning my weight casually into the leather seat of my bike. "Ruins all the fun."

"You want me to go on that?"

"That?" I asked, turning to look in the direction she was looking.

"That," she said, pointing directly under the cheeks of my butt with emphasis.

I once again hid a burgeoning smile. "That's a motorcycle. And, seeing as it's my chosen mode of transportation … yeah."

"I can't," she said quickly, looking to her car to me and back again.

"Why?" I asked, following the trail of her eyes with my own and stopping on her flushed face.

Her brows pulled slightly together, but it wasn't in confusion. It was in search of an excuse. "Because I shouldn't."

"Okay," I agreed. She relaxed, dropping her arms to her side and staring. I took in her markedly less confrontational posture and couldn't resist trying one more time. "Just ..."

She rolled her eyes.

"One more question?"

She nodded her permission, skeptical but listening.

"How do you know you shouldn't?"

Distress lined the corners of her eyes, looking eerily like the narrow end of a spider web, as she fought to maintain her normal detached interest.

"I ... I ..."

My heart thudded in my chest and clamminess formed a pond in the palm of my hand.

"I can't."

Unfamiliar disappointment cracked in my chest and splintered all the way into my gut. I normally did far better with hope management. Today had me all fucked up.

There was no reason to push her though.

"Okay."

She looked disappointed.

Not in me. *In herself.*

Lifting the corners of my mouth into an easy smile, I sought to put her at ease.

"I'll see you tomorrow, then. What time do you like to get started?"

Perhaps surprised to have someone else relying on and managing their life off of her schedule, it took her several seconds to think it through. "I come in pretty early to help out with office work. Condition around noon, take a short lunch break and then start event work and drills."

"I'll be here at one then."

"Okay."

I almost balked at the simplicity with which she agreed, but I was done contemplating for the night. I needed a break and clarity and to not overanalyze every single encounter.

I hoped a good night's sleep would teach me how to do that.

With a nod-salute combination I'd never even considered trying to pull off in my entire life, I turned to my bike, simultaneously shut my eyes in frustration and grabbed my helmet, slapped it on my head, and climbed astride.

It took effort, but I managed not to look back.

Okay. Everything was A-fucking—

CHAPTER FIVE

Callie

Okay.

I thought I'd known, but I'd actually had no idea.

Nik, Nikolai Bagrov, *whatever* … was a pretty big fucking deal. He wasn't just "a power tumbler." He was considered third best in the world.

The *world*.

Like, the entirety of Earth.

I didn't waste time when I got home, rushing to my computer to let Google school me on my lack of knowledge.

And boy, had it. It told me to the tune of sixty YouTube videos and six thousand search results.

Every click of my mouse had me asking one thing over and over again.

Why the hell was he even remotely interested in *coaching* me?

Coaching anybody, really. He should have been training all the time. Living … well … *my life.*

The more I watched and read about him, careful to keep to career facts only rather than personal information, the more I started to relate to him. I didn't want to know about his personal life.

No, that wasn't true.

I didn't want to know unless he told me himself. It felt like an invasion of privacy, and more than that, like I might unearth something I wasn't equipped to handle.

Raised in the life, he'd started tumbling at the ripe age of four and never, ever stopped. A brief foray into Men's gymnastics proved uninteresting at which point he turned all of his energy into tumbling. Building an early career, competing in as many competitions as possible, and largely dominating all that he entered. He'd made several trips to the World Championships, his last one putting him impressively on the podium for bronze.

But watching him tonight, I couldn't help but think he was maybe even better than third in the world. That he could achieve even better if he wanted to.

It was different, but not enough to not be the same. I felt like Nik knew where I was coming from in a completely different way than anyone I'd met before.

Which freaked me the hell out. Relating led to liking, and liking led to losing my mind—and a good chance of disappointment.

It was around the ninth full body shiver that I decided something had to be done. Something preemptive and preventative, and it had to happen now.

With two clicks of the mouse, I pulled up a picture of him and proceeded to pick it apart.

Lips—fucking awesome.

Eyes—unreal. So blue, so water-like, they invited you to dive right in.

Smile—to die for.

But his hair was kind of stupid.

No.

I strengthened my resolve.

Not kind of stupid. It was the *epitome* of stupid. All floppy and long and mop-like in structure. And the whole headband thing was a mockery against men.

Yeah. That was better.

And the motorcycle. That was stupid too!

What was he thinking taking chances getting hurt like that? They were deathtraps.

I mean, it was a *little* hot.

My fingers pinched close to one another in example, and one eye narrowed as I talked to myself.

A skosh.

Admitting to a skosh was totally acceptable, I reasoned.

My head tilted thoughtfully to the side, and the shape of my lips pursed into a heart.

His hair really wasn't *that* bad.

Immediate realization of my backpedaling thoughts made my head snap back to straight.

Shit.

Exiting out of my browser quickly and shoving away from the computer, I hung my head in my hands.

I was just tired. That was all. It was going on one thirty in the morning, and my self-imposed bedtime was a memory.

I still lived with my parents, which, quite frankly, grated, but I knew they had been soundly sleeping for hours at this point. And that kind of ruled out slamming things around the kitchen in a confused rage while mixing a batch of cookie batter to eat straight from the bowl.

So sleep was the answer. Everything would feel normal again tomorrow, surely.

A team picture from my Level Seven days looked on from my dresser top as I let my freshly showered hair out of the confines of its ponytail, stripped off my sweatshirt, and climbed under the down, white comforter on my bed.

With nothing but a lean and a flick of my wrist, the light of my bedside lamp extinguished and plunged the quiet room into nearly complete darkness. The moon shone a sliver of light through my dormer window and settled it directly on the clasp of my hands.

Slowly, I turned them over and studied them, the angry red divots left in the absence of skin and the ugly yellowing of years worth of hardened callouses standing out against the rest of the pale expanse.

I tried to follow the lines of my palm prints, having read in an article online once that the shape of them said something about you as a person.

Try as I might, I couldn't remember what the writer had said.

I imagined, though, for a woman like me, the lines broken by scars and bloody holes and the would-be curves covered by ugly, thickened, abused skin—the answer wouldn't be good.

"Good morning, Callie," my mom called from the sink as I entered the kitchen at the pace of a snail the next morning.

For having only completed what amounted to half of a normal workout for myself, I was worn the fuck out.

Apparently, a day and night full of foreign thoughts and emotions had worked all kinds of mental muscles I had no idea I had. And just like any change in routine, the aftermath was fraught with fatigue and sore.

"Morning, mom."

She turned at the sound of my voice and immediately zeroed in on the dark, unflattering circles under my drooping eyes.

"You look tired."

"Yep."

"You sound tired too."

Shaking my head at the ground, I sighed.

"That's because I *am* tired."

She frowned just as my dad came through the door behind me. He heard the conversation, just as it seemed like he always did, and saw it as his opportunity to take it in the direction that he wanted— another common theme for him.

"That's not good, Cal," he preached, moving toward the table and into my line of sight. "You know this is the homestretch. You've got just under six weeks before Trials and eight until camp."

And ten before the Olympics.

"I know."

I definitely fucking knew.

"You don't eat the way you should," he pointed out just as I reached for a plate with syrup-soaked french toast on it, "and you haven't been putting effort into your conditioning like you should."

"I know," I said, stopping mid reach and retracting my arm obediently.

I *always* said.

"Frank—" my mom attempted to cut in, but he just kept talking.

"Hopefully Nik can teach you some work ethic in this short amount of time."

I fought the downturn of my lips, but I sure as shit didn't win.

"You should have told me you hired a new coach for me."

He looked mystified. "I thought that's what I did yesterday?"

My mom shook her head along with me. *Men.*

"Oh come on. It's not like he's some old guy. He's a really talented tumbler. Maybe you'll even become friends."

I could practically hear the scoff of disbelief as he said it.

"Anyway, I didn't seek him out."

43

I looked to my mom in confusion, but she didn't know what he was talking about either.

She shook her head before turning back to the sink.

"I don't get it. Why's he here then?"

"Friend of a friend thing," he muttered, stabbing his own piece of French toast and bringing it to his mouth. A couple of chews cleared his mouth enough that he could talk.

"You know the Callhoun's? They have the gym up in Moswego?"

Moswego Elite was a competitive gym about two hours north of Ringwood. More backwoods southern Georgia, less coastal small town. I'd been doing competitions with and against them since I was little.

"Yeah."

"Well, they heard from one of their friends that Nik was looking to come on staff at a gym somewhere around here. Something with his parents and having to move or I don't know. Like I said, kind of a grapevine of information."

I wondered briefly at what the story behind all of that half information was, but my dad didn't give me long to think on it, moving on swiftly to his next thought.

"But, anyway, they took him on for a while, said he had a real eye for all of the women's apparatuses even without extensive hands on experience. They didn't have a spot to keep him on permanently, so they called me to check in."

That made my brows pull together too, the idea of a permanent position at our gym ridiculous too. Working with me, at least, would be a very limited time thing. I was already in the homestretch.

"We really don't need anybody, but once I did the research on him, I couldn't turn him away. He's the third ranked power tumbler in the world, you know?"

My mom's head whipped back to the conversation once more.

"I know," I admitted sheepishly. My dad didn't notice.

"After watching him yesterday, I realized he'd be perfect for help-ing you. You know, make him work really hard for his money," he ribbed.

After yesterday?

I didn't laugh.

"Frank," my mom admonished.

"What?"

"Nothing, Dad," I cut in, just wanting this conversation to end. "I have to go. I'm gonna grab an egg white sandwich on the way in to open."

My dad smiled proudly.

There was no fucking way I was getting an egg white sandwich.

I knew I shouldn't encourage him by catering to him in these conversations, but he was like a dog with a bone. His way wasn't the right way. It was the *only* way.

If I didn't cave, he'd go at me until I did.

Don't get me wrong, my dad was a nice guy. He didn't yell at me or hit me. He didn't even withhold love. I had all of the good stuff, and frankly, I was twenty-six and I'd yet to see pressure to contribute more financially or pull more weight. I worked at the gym doing of-fice work in the mornings and worked on my gymnastics the rest of the time. That was good with him.

But that was all good with him because it was what *he* wanted.

I wasn't just his daughter. I was his Olympian.

And he made sure I never forgot it.

The hands of the clock moved lethargically, seemingly struggling to tick from one minute to the next all morning.

I worked to busy my hands and mind, collecting checks from all-too-eager parents, and filing several updated medical release forms. Some of the homeschooled gymnasts trickled in little by little, gabbing and gossiping with each other and glancing my way fearfully as they did.

When noontime finally rolled around, I couldn't get out of the desk chair and out to my car fast enough.

Pulling open my glove box, I checked to make sure I had the air freshener—I did—and then fired it up and pulled out of the parking lot. I had to get out before my dad got in or I never would.

McDonald's lit up like a beacon twelve blocks later, and I flicked the turn signal on in my Honda Civic with avid anticipation.

Everything felt good. I executed a perfect parking job in a spot close to the door. The sun shone vibrantly, warming my bones and radiating outward. And the line inside looked blessedly short.

Apparently, my good mood made me oblivious to the shiny motorcycle parked three spaces down from me.

I awoke swiftly at the sight of Nik, though. Floppy, ugly black hair tucked discreetly under an all black, backwards facing ball cap, well-fitting jeans, and another bright white t-shirt practically slammed their way into my vision like a brick wall.

And unfortunately, he noticed me just as speedily.

"Hey."

Panicked, I immediately accused him of the nearly impossible. "Did my dad send you here? How does he know I'm here?"

He looked around briefly, understandably confused, before excusing himself out of line and approaching me where I'd frozen the moment I'd spotted him.

When he got within two feet, my already tight body strung even tighter.

"I don't know what you're talking about, Callie. I'm here for a Quarter Pounder." I relaxed for a second ... until I realized how embarrassing my whole episode was.

He shrugged. "I would have snuck you in line too, let you order with me, but you kind of stopped moving."

"My dad … " I searched for words, "doesn't like when I eat McDonald's."

Understatement.

"Oh," he breathed through a smile. "Well, your secret's safe with me."

I very nearly smiled back. "Thanks."

He shrugged. And then *winked.*

Sweet good gracious.

"We've all got secrets, right?"

I sure as hell did. By supposition, I assumed everyone else did too.

"Yeah."

I just wondered how many people's secrets were of omission and how many were—

CHAPTER SIX

Nik

Lies.

They aren't always intentional. And sometimes, we only tell them to others because we first tell them to ourselves.

Likewise, pictures aren't always what they seem to be on the surface. Ninety percent of perception is influence, and Callie had perfectly persuaded me to see her role in the gym how she did. Unwanted and resented and well past idolized.

But the more I watched her, the more I learned.

Each snub she felt was fictitious, each sneer a vivid falsity concocted only by her own self-esteem issues.

These kids still idolized and watched her, but her cold, uninterested vibe held them at bay and forced wide-eyed wonderment to hide within side-eyed glances.

I'd have to figure out a way to shift her view and unveil theirs.

After the way yesterday had gone, I knew that I would need to plan for it to be a time-consuming endeavor. There was no hope of convincing her in a single day—especially not this early on in the game.

The right time would eventually come.

"Good," I called as she landed her layout at the end of her series on beam.

She flashed one quick, cocky—thrilled—smile in my direction.

We'd already practiced the other three events, and I'd been relentlessly critical. I'd been surprised to find her teeth still intact when she opened her mouth, her agitated grinding had been so relentless.

But this—this was something different.

She handled beam more confidently than any other event, it seemed, ignoring the danger of fours (four inches wide and four feet tall) with the ease of a tightrope walker. I didn't have all that much experience in this apparatus, but every female gymnast I'd ever encountered—including my mom—talked about it like it was the bane of their existence. And I had enough practical knowledge to know what looked good and didn't.

But Callie wasn't like the others.

She seemed at home there, the soft thump of her landings resonating with precision. There were no sloppy stumbles, no unsure missteps.

When she was on beam, she just *was*.

A few artistic steps led into a full turn, her leg raised and extended well past the end of its execution, and finished with the flourish of an impossibly flexible arabesque. Her eyes zeroed in on the end of the beam in front of me, and the toe of her extended leg tapped the back end of the beam intentionally on its descent. It was a safety measure, a pretty way of ensuring proper positioning on a limited-length beam before her dismount. But, as I'd learned today, she did it with practiced regularity, and she *did it beautifully*.

I could hardly take my eyes off of her.

She had talent in dance and artistic movement in a way that not all gymnasts did. Fluid motion came naturally, and transitions from one skill into another bled as seamlessly as a singular thought being strung together.

My breath caught as she executed her round off, her hands leaving the beam several moments before being replaced by her feet. Precision was key on the round off before a difficult dismount. One mistake or misplaced foot could set a chain of unstoppable disaster in motion.

Once you started a dismount off of the Beam, you really couldn't stop.

A loud thwack rent the air as her feet planted themselves on the mat, knocking my held breath out of my overinflated lungs.

Screams and cheers echoed in the background from the younger team girls on floor from some other noteworthy performance as she turned to approach me, but I ignored them.

Callie's eyes were smug and challenging at once, and I couldn't look away as the light reflected to make the normally hard chocolate look melted.

"Well?"

She obviously thought I was only there to be critical.

"You were incredible," I admitted immediately, painting her face with surprise and bewilderment. "If you were like that on everything, I wouldn't need to be here."

She rolled her eyes, their warmth cooling a little with resentment. "You just had to bring it back to the negative side, huh?"

Uncrossing my arms from my chest and reaching out, I grabbed her shoulder gently and shook amiably back and forth. "No. That was absolutely not meant to be a dig. You're incredible to watch on beam. Comfortable and sure and completely settled inside of your skin."

Just her eyes smiled as I rounded the conversational corner to my point.

"You don't look that way anywhere else," I stated matter-of-factly. "And watching it just now … I couldn't take my eyes off of you."

She shrugged sheepishly at the compliment, unsure how to handle it. A flush stole across her features and her hands fidgeted in front of her.

"It's always been that way. I'm just comfortable here." One corner of her dusty pink lips tipped up in thought. "Happy, I guess."

My eyes narrowed, and my curiosity piqued.

"And you're not happy on Bars, Vault, and Floor?"

Her spine straightened as her admission cleared the fog, and her face slammed closed once more.

"That's not what I said."

I wanted to delve into the reasoning behind everything she'd said and the sensitive way with which she reacted.

But raucous sounds from behind me interrupted and curtailed my thoughts.

"1, 2, 3, GO GYMSTARS!" we heard screamed from the floor. The group made a clean break but dispersed unevenly from there, some heading for the locker room and others the front or the bathroom up front.

For me, it was a cue of opportunity. What opportunity, I wasn't sure. I kept telling myself I just wanted to get to know her better so I could be a better coach, but each statement held less and less professional conviction and, instead, built an abundance of uninvited personal investment.

Knowing didn't seem to stop me though.

"You want to hang out tonight while I tumble?"

Her head whipped back to me, the long glossy tail of her hair cutting through the air like an expertly wielded sword.

"What?"

"I just asked if you want to—"

She shook her head rapidly. "I know what, I guess. I meant why. *Why* are you asking me to stay?"

I didn't have a good answer. I knew I shouldn't and at the same time I couldn't stop myself. Instead, I shrugged. "Because I can't think of a good enough reason not to."

The line was getting slicker by the minute, the feel of it slipping out from underneath my dangerously treading feet oddly enjoyable. As a guy who lived most of his life on the opposite side of that line, I couldn't even begin to understand what was happening.

All I knew was that I liked it.

She searched the gym with her eyes and landed on the locker room. Back they came to me once more, and then back to the locker room.

This time their movement was slower, but it was infinitely more confident.

An unhurried smile crept onto her normally taut lips as she teased, "Are you any good?"

I couldn't stop my cheeks from lifting as I replied, weaving my head back and forth between my shoulders as I did. "A couple people are better."

"Just a couple?" she pushed as if she knew.

I narrowed my eyes, trying to see the proof that she'd looked into me written somewhere legible and obvious, but settled for a brisk nod when the search came up predictably empty.

Straight white teeth cut a soft line into the line of her bottom lip. They weren't plump or overfilled. They were just normal. And plenty damn pretty.

"Then I guess I'll stay."

"Yeah?"

"Yep. I'm gonna need you to prove your skill to me."

White hot lust shot down my spine and into my balls at the double entendre in her words. I knew she hadn't meant it. She didn't even realize the blunder herself.

But my dick had been noticing lots. The innuendo and her body and the way a touch to her shoulder fired my nerves better than the well-placed touch of an experienced woman.

"I … Ah … Um … Yes … Okay," I stuttered. In actuality, I was impressed. As much as I'd struggled, my brain had done the talking despite the death grip my dick had on my voice box.

Shaking my head and my thoughts, I tried to talk myself off the ledge of self-sabotage and back to the land of reality.

This woman was a gymnast I coached. I was her *coach*, for fuck's sake. It would be totally douchey of me to exert my power and influence as a figure of trust in her life in order to get in her pants.

Leotard.

Fuck. *No.*

I wasn't getting inside of anything.

"Nik?" she called, focusing my attention on something other than the brain versus biology war being fought in my head. My brain used logic and strategy and well-placed task forces to talk me around to the right side of battle, but strategy didn't mean much when biology bombed the living hell out of my synapses.

"Sorry. What'd you say?"

"Ummmm," she said, sounding perplexed. "Nothing. Just your name."

"Oh. Okay."

"For the last minute and a half."

Well that's embarrassing.

"Sorry, I was … thinking."

Explicit thinking was still thinking.

"Alright, well, everyone else is packing up and getting ready to leave, so I'm gonna go change."

"You're not going to tumble with me?"

"What? No! I'm not even in the same league as you." Covering, she added, "I wouldn't imagine I am anyway. I'll just watch."

"Come on, tumble with me."

"No—"

"Callie."

"Nik."

"*Callie.*"

"*Nik.*"

"Callie," I said once more, knowing that if you held out long enough, people normally became annoyed enough to give in.

"Okay! Fine! I won't change!"

The last stragglers of the night looked on with avid interest as they crossed the floor to the exit.

"Yelling is kind of becoming our thing, you know?" I offered, ignoring their nameless faces and smiling at hers.

"Shut up," she snipped playfully.

"No, really. I don't even think they'll call us by name soon. We'll just be 'those people who yell.'"

She tilted her head forward and raised a brow in disgust.

A warning.

I kept talking anyway, standing proudly with my hands on my hips. "The Yellertons."

I stumbled and tripped, the result of her shove catching me off guard.

"What?" she asked when I looked at her with surprised hostility. "Now they can call us 'the people who shove each other.'"

"Cute," I laughed, adjusting my hair by pushing it out of my face.

"One of us has to be," she poked in jest, shoving a finger in my direction as if plotting a poke in my chest.

"Whatever," I mocked, hands to my forehead in the shape of a 'w'.

"Go change!" she demanded, throwing her hands forward in the direction of the bathroom. "Unless you've changed your mind and don't intend to tumble?"

I threw up both hands in useless defense and backed slowly toward the exit. "Alright, alright. Relax. I have to go get my bag."

An unexpected chill hit me as I shoved through the door into the warm, muggy air of a Southern Georgia summer night. I could hear the echoes of my flirtation following me the entire walk to my motorcycle, and my euphoria skirted the edge of dismay and back again.

It felt good to want something.

But why did I have to want something I shouldn't?

Frustrated and flustered, I snapped open the saddlebag in a rush, grabbed my bag, and nearly slammed it shut.

My feet itched to jog on the way back, but I forced them to walk, the anticipation roiling rigorously between sour and sweet in my gut with each step.

The door felt lighter on the swing to enter, but I didn't seek out the cause. Instead I headed straight for the bathroom and changed quickly, doing all of the necessary taping and preparation that I always did.

When I exited to the gym, the lights were down except for the one we needed, and Callie lounged on the end of the rod floor with her legs extended in front of her and crossed at the ankles with the weight of her trim body settled into her forearms behind her back.

My bag hit the ground just in time to set off her giggles.

Hunched and pressed into herself, her stomach muscles contracted with each peal, and her toes curled until they folded backwards into the floor.

"What?" I asked, knowing the object of her laughter had to be me, but at a loss for the exact reason why.

"Nothing," she avoided.

"What?" I persisted.

She rolled her eyes and gave in, sitting up slowly as she did.

"It's just … your hair. It's … well, it's—"

"Funny," I finished for her.

That didn't stop her from getting the last word, a cute scrunch of her nose cushioning the effect of her words. "Looking. It's funny looking."

"Thanks?"

"Oh," she said in realization, squealing her laughter to an immediate halt. "Sorry."

I didn't want to make her feel bad. It wasn't like this was the in-style and I'd perfectly crafted it to look this way. It was just a convenient fact like a million other things I hadn't bothered to change.

"No worries. I'm not particularly fond of it or anything. Just haven't put any effort in to cut it in the last six months or so."

"And the headband?" she questioned with a flick of her dainty chin.

My eyes rolled up as though I could see it atop my head. "It's just practical." I shrugged. "Messes with my tumbling if it gets in my eyes."

Her cheeks pinked as she nodded in reply. The rosy color softened her eyes again, and I had to turn to my phone to keep from getting distracted by them.

Finding the song more easily than the night before, I turned up the volume, dropped it to my bag, pulled my shirt over my head and walked over to the end of the floor with Callie.

She scrambled up quickly, moving out of my way as though too close of a proximity would result in an electric shock.

And hell, maybe she was right.

"Metallica?" she asked with surprising musical knowledge. I, on the other hand, knew very little. I only knew this music because it had been ingrained in me from the time I could listen.

"Yeah," I confirmed before admitting, "My dad's favorite band."

"Oh."

"Yeah," I chuckled, the memory of my mom yelling at my dad to listen to something with an actual melody making me smile. "My mom hated it too."

I could picture her face so perfectly in my mind, the way she nagged and nagged at my dad to find something better to love. He always told her he already had. And, as their child, I normally left the room thoroughly grossed out.

"I don't hate it," Callie qualified. "It's just intense. Kind of makes my heart feel like it's going to beat out of my chest."

I pulled myself out of my nostalgia and focused fully on her and her explanation.

"Funny. That's what makes me like it."

The dichotomy of our opinions of the same visceral reaction astonished me.

"Really?" she asked, putting a hand flat to her chest to feel the effect the music had on each beat.

"Definitely," I confirmed, putting a single hand to my own chest and harnessing it. "It's perfect tumbling music."

"Why?"

I shrugged. To me, the reasoning was simple. "Music feeds power, and tumbling thrives off of it." I searched my brain quickly and came up empty. "I can't think of a more symbiotic relationship actually."

"Not even peanut butter and jelly?"

"No way," I denied. "Compared to music and tumbling, it's like peanut butter fucking hates jelly."

A small laugh of disbelief bounded out of her throat like a cough, but the tide of consideration rolled in slowly and changed it to interested acceptance.

"Teach me your ways," she offered easily, a smile curving the corners of her mouth fully this time and completely transforming her face while one hand gestured gallantly to the floor.

This.

God, I'd have to recreate it. Every night if I could.

Her personality morphed into a less structured version of itself and her figurative hair came down.

She was—

CHAPTER SEVEN

Callie

Relaxed.

It went that way for the next three weeks straight. Workouts swung from high to low as he criticized or praised, and my favorite time to be in the gym stayed very much the same.

But the company was oh so different than it had been for the majority of my life.

Sometimes we meshed and sometimes we didn't, but we found a rhythm and routine. And I finally admitted to myself that I was happy to have him there—no matter how mixed up and jumbled he had my emotions.

He pushed, and I pushed back.

Somehow though, we managed to do it without knocking one another down.

Every night when we walked out of the building together, sweaty with laughter and endorphins buzzing deliriously from the exercise, he asked me to go somewhere with him.

Every night I said no.

But as he turned to me with hope in his handsome blue eyes, his stupid hair tucked away beneath his backward hat, I felt my tongue change direction. I fought it tooth and nail, scrapping and scraping and scratching at the image of my fleeting sanity.

I had my obsession with him managed at this point, but it carved a very tenuous edge. One I knew could be sharpened to the point of irreparable damage with just one night of recklessness.

"Callie."

"Nik—" I started to say, very much knowing where he was going and needing to fight myself for conviction.

His eyes widened just slightly, the sad look of a puppy at the pound begging for a savior, weakening me at the knees and threatening to display all of my carefully hidden goo.

"Come with me. *Please.*"

The "please" sealed my coffin, each succulent letter driving in like an individual nail intending to secure my capture.

As the first syllable of my answer left my lips his face reacted minutely, hard jaws flanking a set of pinched pillow-like lips, but it wasn't to the word I said.

It was to the one he expected.

"Alright."

He nodded, forcing a gulp through his frustrated throat.

"One day you're going to say ... wait ... did you just say alright?" he replied, stumbling over the words in a messy mix of confusion and excitement and screeching his upset nod to a halt.

"I did," I confirmed with a smirk.

His entire body came alive, kind of how it did before a tumbling pass, energy passing through his fingers and toes and shooting plainly out of his anything-but-plain eyes.

It was boy-like in nature but mature in appearance, and with each second I soaked it in, I knew that the anticipation of my constant 'nos' had made a one time 'yes' that much better.

For him *and* for me.

"Good. Good, that's good," he stuttered some more, making my smile deepen.

In fact, it was so enthralling, it kind of made me want to drag out every decision and discussion I ever had, making the other party suffer if only for the good of the outcome.

"Don't even think about it," he warned, reading the illicit intent in my eyes and the mischief in the line of my mouth.

Normally I kept a vise-like grip on my emotions, but I seemed to defy all normality and logic around him. Emotion bled through not only the bone and the flesh within me, but seeped out the pores in my skin and covered him with their sweat.

Any appeal he might find in it I supposed rested in the circumstances of the situation, much how actual sweat garnered magnetism, during a passionate romp, and repugnance, after a vigorous workout, in equal measure.

The differences in my mood were stark, volleying between comfortable enjoyment and unfamiliar distrust.

I couldn't figure out what he had switched on in me, where he found the secret key hidden after it spent so many years collecting undisturbed dust. But proximity left me with no choice but to face it, embracing it a little more each day as all of the previously solitary hours of my days filled with him.

I just wondered if I was at all prepared to handle it. I had no real ruler against which to measure my feelings and reactions or the way he felt about me. I didn't know how to navigate what was appropriate and what wasn't or if any of it even mattered.

I just knew I couldn't stop even if I wanted to.

Time seemed to speed up as he handed me the extra helmet out of his saddle bag and climbed astride as he strapped on his own.

I wasn't sure if my anxiety was playing with my perception of the passing of time or if it actually *was* fast, a desperate method by a man intent on keeping me from changing my mind.

All I knew is that one moment I was saying yes, and the next, I was climbing astride a motorcycle for the first time in my life with little instruction or insight into what I was getting myself into.

Three weeks of familiarity and long surreptitious forays into his eyes had me fairly confident that I wasn't riding straight to my own murder, but other than that I knew nothing. I still had no personal information about his background or family or what had brought him here. His likes could be extrapolated from genuine smiles and warm excitement, but outside of gymnastics and tumbling, I hadn't had all that much to apply it to.

And as someone who'd had her future mapped from the first few, not entirely clumsy, toddler steps, the notion of going in blind both boiled and iced over in the pit of my very unsure stomach.

"Nik," I called as he started the bike and pulled my arms around his taut stomach.

His hand covered mine, and the feel of his fingers sliding through mine started to calm the riotous waters within before he even started to speak.

"Don't worry, Cal," he assured me, calling me by a nickname only ever used by my father. The sound of it from his endearing lips made fast work of changing it into something sought after rather than protected against. "I promise you're going to love it."

I rolled my eyes, and he laughed at the same time, clarifying, "Or, at the very least, live through it and feel no regret from having been there."

He squeezed my hand again, and then lifted his hands to the grips, revving the throttle in a teasing exhibition of potential danger and releasing the clutch until we lurched forward in a slow roll.

A squeal escaped my lips uninhibited, and the muscles of his abdomen shook under my hand.

He turned right out of the parking lot and headed straight into the darkness of one of the most rural areas of our town, moving at a leisurely enough pace to set me at ease without adding an extra hour to our arrival time.

As first, I held on tight, focusing my eyes on the road like a professional grade laser in order to be prepared for catastrophe or mayhem. But as the minutes ticked by and the vibration between my legs dulled and smoothed out from adjustment, I finally started to settle.

Deep breaths once again passed through my lungs with ease, and the smell of saltwater tickled the tip of my nose with awareness.

"We're heading for the water?" I tried to question over the roar.

I swore I could feel his smile all the way into the line of his body, but he didn't answer.

The exhaust popped a couple of times as he cracked the throttle from open to closed, slowed us to a crawl, and turned off onto a sandy dirt path through a waist-high, grassy field.

I could hear the dull roar of waves, just barely whooshing over the more gravelly hum of his motorcycle.

I couldn't see it, though, as he pulled to a stop at the back of a tall dune and killed the engine.

Silence rang loudly in my noise-expectant ears for the first few seconds, and his hands moved mine from his stomach to his shoulders in a nonverbal prompt to climb off.

I did as he asked, standing on one peg and swinging the other leg over the back of my seat. He followed me as soon as I cleared his space, reaching for my helmet as I unstrapped it and setting it gently on the seat where my butt had been.

When he had his helmet off too, he replaced it with his hat, having worn it nearly constantly since I'd made the comments about his hair, and reached for my hand.

I took it without hesitation, questioning only where we were going—and trusting him to guide me there.

We climbed the dune together with relative ease, but when we reached the top, I felt my breathing labor.

Stretched out before me, a similar path to the one we'd just been on sliced through another willowy, breezy-blown field, yawned into a beach, and led directly to the moonlit ocean. Blue crystals of gulf water seemed to shimmer above the surface, and the sand took on the motion of active glitter. But what really got me were the thousands upon thousands of lightning bugs that danced over the grass of the field, mirroring the luster of the sand and the ocean and perfectly tying together the fantastical location.

Nik waited patiently through my silence, doing nothing but squeezing my hand as a gasp of air escaped my lips.

"What is this place?"

"Well, I guess technically, it's Riley Beach. The last place I know of this close to the ocean to have lightning bugs."

I knew nothing about the habitat of lightning bugs, but his words suggested significance. I settled for believing him.

I shook my head in answer to my wonder, but I didn't look at him—or away from the picture in front of me.

"But to me, it's the place I come to feel close to my parents."

"Why does this place make you feel close to your parents?" I asked, turning to look at him at the prompting of his tone.

He shrugged, looking out in front of us, and took one deep breath. "Because it's impossible to see them again." My free hand floated to my lips, just as he gripped the one resting in his. "And this place feels like magic."

"*Nik.*"

"They died in a car accident six months ago."

It was fact. It was an admission. It was a functionally large crack in his well-performing heart.

"I'm sorry," I said, pouring my condolences into the two words and moving my hand from my mouth to his, cocooning it with my hands from both sides.

"Me too, Cal," he whispered, moving his eyes from the beach to me. "That's not why I brought you here, though, okay?"

My eyebrows pinched together and my lips lifted closer to my nose.

"I'm sad they're gone. But they didn't miss anything, you know? I'm happy and healthy and they raised me to be a person we're all proud of. They loved each other more than most people think is natural, and they built a life for themselves in a country that wasn't their own. They treated it like it was, though. You know, they never even talked about Russia to me. Never taught me a syllable of Russian, never enforced customs or traditions."

I paid attention, trying to soak in all the things he spoke about with such positive conviction without making my own opposing judgements.

"I know," he said, once again reading my traitorous face. "Trust me, my relatives thought it was crazy too. But see, to me, it was because they didn't see themselves as Russian anymore. They were American, and so was their baby." He shrugged his shoulder. "I'm not saying it was right or wrong, but it *did* make them happy. And now, with them gone what seems like so soon, I'm thankful for that."

"Me too."

Not knowing if I should but doing it anyway, I pushed it, noting, "They sure as hell gave you a Russian sounding name though, Nikolai."

His eyes met mine with a genuine smile, but he didn't make any moves to explain.

I didn't really need him to anyway.

He looked back to the ocean, and I followed suit, but when the silence stretched on, I asked a different question that was still unanswered.

"So, why did you bring me here?"

He looked into my eyes again, searching them and my face with an intensity that twisted my insides and lifted my heart as if on a platter.

Another shrug lifted the line of his shoulders, but it wasn't because he didn't know. It was a gesture of admission.

"To share it with you."

I felt uncomfortably cornered, the honesty in his eyes and the soft stroke of his thumb on the back of my hand lulling me into some sort of alternate universe where I was supposed to feel this way for my coach.

His eyes left mine to travel to my lips, and I could feel the pull as my body swayed in an effort to give in.

It was dangerous and tempting, and I scrambled to distract myself with questions that didn't necessarily need answers.

"Why isn't anyone else here? Isn't this the sort of place that would attract a crowd?"

"Most people don't go to the trouble to find it," he explained, illustrating his point by asking, "How long have you lived here?"

"Point taken." And it was. I lived a solid seven miles from here, and I'd never known it existed. I'd gone from one place to another on a plan without any attempts to wander.

"And those of us who do know, don't ever tell," he whispered, a wink traveling slowly through the iris of his eye like a wave through the nearby ocean.

"Shhh," he breathed, the warm air from his mouth sending a shiver across my cheek. "Best kept secret in Southern Georgia."

I wasn't so sure.

Because hidden in the depths of my pounding chest, controlled by the softness of his eyes and the warmth of his larger than life smile was one *very* secret thing.

Something I had to fight to keep at bay, when I lay awake at night, when I watched the flare of his eyes, and under the watchful vision of my father and everyone else involved in not only my destiny, but his—

CHAPTER EIGHT

Want.

Rampant and wild and nearly unchecked, it flowed through my veins like adrenaline and only spiked as each annoying moment of this day ticked on.

The frustration of my unsatisfied longing crept into my coaching as I watched her run through her routine with the same indifference she'd been shoving on me since we'd parted ways last night.

Both things were false and contrived, and I could tell she had to actually *work* at not caring. Her toes only pointed in half measures, and the extension of her core was completely lacking. She sank into herself instead of pulling herself up out of the Beam, and the effect on her appeal was deadening.

Her. The same woman who'd enthralled and enraptured me with her movement on this apparatus for the three weeks prior.

Deep breathing before her dismount, a small line of concentration formed between her arched brows for the first time. Minimal effort put in only when needed.

I was supremely underwhelmed, and for as fascinating as I found her to watch, that was really saying something. The judges would be even less impressed if she didn't dig deep enough to find some heat. All traces of its previous existence had vanished, the spoils of her effort nothing more than a plastic, lifeless veneer.

As soon as her feet hit the mat, I found my voice. It echoed in the mostly empty, large space, and, still used to being the only one in her world, she jumped at the first syllable.

"Great. Now how about you try doing that routine like you mean it," I boomed. Her narrowed eyes whipped to mine and my voice turned garbled with gravel. "Like it means something to you." I held her eyes with the contempt of a child robbed of his favorite toy, knowing on some instinctual level that this was all about me. "Because that version was *completely* devoid of passion. You look like you're out for a stroll through the grocery store!"

"Who needs passion when you've got more than enough for the both of us?" she snapped in reaction to the crack of my angry voice, stalking from the mat to me and looking menacingly into my face.

"Lower your voice, for God's sake," she instructed through gritted teeth.

"What's going on with you?" I asked, lowering my volume painstakingly and pointedly.

"You're like a different person today. Cold and detached, and it shows in every move you make." I couldn't stop the hurt from seeping slightly into my voice.

"That," she accused in an agitated whisper, her pointed finger aimed directly at my face. "*That* right there. That's why I can't be open and uninhibited. You make that fucking face, and I nearly forget how to put my left foot in front of my right. And Olympians can't afford to miss a single goddamn step."

I tried to rein in the anger and embrace her admission instead. She felt what I felt around her in the same confusing swirl.

Calming my attack and considering my words, I tried to explain that not everything was black and white.

"Being strong doesn't mean you can't be soft. Working hard to meet your goals doesn't mean you can't live. And living a certain way your entire life doesn't mean you can't ever change. Life is fluid. The only way to run yourself ashore is to not follow the change and contour of the curves."

She shook her head, frustrated.

She wasn't the only one.

"Listen, Nik. It's like this." We'd crept incredibly close to one another at this point, the rest of the gym a memory. Her anger and mine filled the space around us, and her hands moved to illustrated her point as if playing a game of charades.

"I'm already on one high-speed boat, throttle wide open, and the steering wheel pegged. It doesn't matter if I want to be on another fucking boat, the leap *isn't worth the risk*."

My chest blew back, and my mind reeled that the possibility that she actually thought that was how life worked. That you worked and bled and sweat for one goddamn thing, and any time you wanted anything else you had to choose between it and your fucking life.

"So, what? You're only allowed to have one thing?" I asked, the concept completely ridiculous in my mind.

"When it takes as much work and doing as this?" Her face and nod were resolute. "Yes."

I shook me head, resisting the urge to pull out my hair by locking my hands onto my hips. "With all you're doing, how do you ever make time to dream?"

"Dreamers are weak-willed," she stated, turning her head away from me and focusing out to the side rather than facing the scrutiny of my eyes. "Instead of working toward concrete goals, they get lost

70

in the fantasy of expectation. I don't think about what I'm going to do. I just do it."

I softened my voice and attitude, hoping to pull her eyes back in line with mine. "Weak willed doesn't mean weak-minded." Her head turned back slowly. "Dreamers use every facet of their mind, so much so, their will can't resist."

The weight of our conversation sagged the line of her shoulders and pulled at the length of her slim neck. Her posture changed from angry to subdued, and trapped under the watchful eyes of an entire gym full of people, I couldn't do one thing about it.

But as her eyes lifted to meet mine, soft and warm but stagnant, I realized that was exactly what she wanted.

A public scene meant limitations, and yelling between us was expected.

It was our thing.

"I'm sorry," she whispered, stabbing me in the heart with one of the most brutal non-breakups I'd ever had.

I'd never have her the way I wanted, and this was her way of delivering the blow.

Part of me understood. I knew the world she lived in, the expectations she so painstakingly tried to live up to.

But another part of me didn't get it at all, the ability to resist what was happening between us, a connection so real it had formed the moment I'd taken her spit-soaked hand.

And that was the part I would have to find a way to live with.

I didn't want to let her down professionally, but getting into that mindset was going to take some reflection and convincing.

"I think I'm done for today," I admitted, using her words from that first night unintentionally and taking a step back.

"Nik—"

"I just need the day, Callie. I'll be back tomorrow."

Fighting the urge to say more, she nodded and backed away as

I turned to go.

Coaches and gymnasts alike stared as I left, but I plastered a fake smile on my face and waved as I went.

I would never jeopardize anything for Callie based on a dredged up personal issue.

"Nik!" Frank called as I passed the office and forcing me to a stop. He was truly the last person I wanted to talk to in that moment.

"Yes, sir?" I forced out in a fake show of casualness.

"Leaving early?"

"Uh, yeah," I admitted, lying my way through an explanation. "I have an appointment."

He studied me closely, and I increased the wattage of my smile in answer.

"Callie can be tough—"

"No, sir," I cut in.

He raised his eyebrows in disbelief.

My lungs puffed a huge gust of air, forcing it up my throat and out my mouth. I used it to breath life into my answer. "I mean, yes, she can be confrontational—"

He laughed.

I fought the narrowing of my eyes.

"But this isn't about her, sir. Just an appointment. I'll be back tomorrow."

His eyes were curious, but he didn't push. "Alright then. Have a good evening."

"Thank you. You too."

Air screamed freedom, and I couldn't get out the door to breathe it in fast enough.

My chest felt sore, and I raised a hand to rub it as I walked quickly to my Street Glide. Normally I made sure to change into my jeans before I got on the bike, but I didn't have it in me to go back in, so I just left it.

I felt more alone than I had in a while, the knowledge of each friend and relationship secondary to the loss of one thing when it came to Callie—

CHAPTER NINE

Callie

Hope.

It spread like an infection and tainted clean vision and dedication. It made me think about, and long for, other things outside of the one thing that encapsulated my entire life.

The fact was, I didn't know how to be anything other than this, I didn't know how to strive for something other than greatness, and the prospect of the consequences forced my hand with the cure.

Hurting Nik yesterday had physically hurt me, the figurative gaping hole in my chest lacking the ability to clot. It had taken everything in me not to go after him, to let it go—to convince myself that it was all for the best.

I hadn't specifically tried to aggravate him, but I hadn't been naive enough to think it wouldn't happen either. Part of me thought I needed the scene, the whole argument to make a clean break and go back to what practice and experience told me was important. But it didn't heal all of the longing and wonderment in me. If anything, it made me rage to understand its unavoidable pull even harder.

It still felt fresh to me today, and I knew he felt the same. His words weren't bitter, but they were cutting, the struggle he was feeling apparently just as real as my own.

Mud clouded the pristine water of his eyes, and all the ease had vanished from his posture.

He moved with stilted agitation, and I couldn't even blame him because I was doing the same thing.

The difference was, he and everyone else were judging me based on mine.

If he told me I was jerking to one skill from another in my bar routine instead of flowing one more time, I was going to punch him in the throat.

Granted, half of my frustration came from him and the other half came from the inability to complete this stupid, godforsaken skill.

"You're releasing too late. There's no way you'll be able to grab the bar doing it like that. Look down the line of your body, when your toes point right there," he pointed to the joint between the ceiling and the wall, "that's when you let go."

"I know," I grated, smashing my lips together and checking the tightness of my grips on my wrists.

"If you know, do it."

His anger fueled mine, riling us up into a torturous circle of aggression.

"Relax, alright?" I snapped. "This is a new fucking skill, and it's taking me a little time to get used to it."

His eyes glittered and shimmered, and the line of his jaw became noticeably more compact.

"If you're this slow to take what you want, I don't know how the hell you expect to take that goddamn podium."

I shook my head at his absurdity, knowing that the guise of gymnastics talk was just that—an emotional ruse. "The two aren't even remotely related."

"How do you figure that?" he asked, slamming his hands to his hips and pretending not to know what I was talking about.

"Because when it comes to gymnastics, I know what it takes. I know that I'm safe."

An outsider would have laughed at the absurdity of that statement. Gymnastics, as a sport, was anything but safe. But Nik knew exactly what I meant.

Because he was living the double meaning along with me, and he saw inside the window to my mind like no one else I'd ever encountered.

Gymnastics was known. It didn't change. It was comfort.

That didn't stop him from refuting my logic.

"I'll make you a promise right here," he swore, his words a conviction and a truth and a vow that he'd do anything to keep. "There are a lot of things you may never be with me, but you'll *always* be fucking safe."

I wanted so badly to give in, to cave to his line of thinking and believe that what he said wouldn't only be a promise, but an irrefutable fact. But I knew better. Years of not getting my way reinforced that it would never change.

"Gymnastics is safe," I told him in an effort to distance him. I needed him to back off from this argument, to let it go. Unless he did, I wouldn't be able to. Not unless he was gone.

"Gymnastics is not supposed to be your *entire* life," he insisted, his face imploring. "You're allowed to have more than this."

He poked and poked the bear inside me until it was cornered, and my only option left was to growl.

"Jesus Christ!" I threw my hands in the air. "What do you think you are, some kind of life coach?! You coach *gymnastics*," I spat, feeling the chords in my throat stand out with each rage filled syllable. "You're here to improve my gymnastics. *That's it.*"

If I'd been expecting an apology or concession, it was nothing but my fault. People were reliably predictable, and Nik wasn't any different. He never apologized or lived regret. He lived that moment, breathed that reasoning, and answered every irrational outburst of mine with a rational calm that blew my mind. I kept to myself, so it was easy to fool people into believing I was low key, but I had never been an even keel kind of person. I blew up and I did it hard, whether it lived completely in my mind or splattered all over everything just depended on who I was dealing with. Every moment with him was infinitely messy.

Those words had drawn what I considered to be a line in the sand. But Nik … he wasn't afraid to cross it.

His chest blew back as if I'd struck him, but it wasn't because he was contrite. It was because he was winding up for a punch that would be anything but physical, but would leave its mark all the same.

"Gymnastics isn't a self contained sport. It's not only the training, only the skills, only the work you put in. It takes mental toughness and adaptability," he annunciated, tapping his temple with rapt precision. "Neither of which work cohesively with a hothead or simmering unhappiness. The more fulfilled your life is, the more your gymnastics will improve."

The corner of his mouth just barely hitched as he rounded the corner of his speech and settled into his exceptionally made point. "So I *am* coaching you at gymnastics. But for you, the area you're lacking in isn't skill or dedication. It's goddamn *life.*"

Without apology or hesitation he was gone, time for a rebuttal completely off the table of accessibility.

I watched numbly as he left, not even slowing for the rain that beat an unrelenting rhythm on the metal roof of the warehouse.

Anger seared hot all over my skin, and as a stroke of worry for the safety of riding his motorcycle in this weather came over me, it burned all the way through like acid.

How dare he come into my life and mess everything up?

Until he rammed his bossy way in, the only person I had to worry about was myself. My safety, my opinions, my feelings, and my goddamn wants.

His words bounced like ping pong balls in my head, catching slightly in the net and making me doubt my own serve. I didn't want to get lost in his fucking speeches and look forward to his smiles. I didn't want to have to worry about him in the rain or the wind or any other godforsaken showing of mother nature.

I hadn't asked for it, hadn't prepared for it, but the bastard had done it all the same.

Unwilling and unable to stop myself, I took off at a run for the door, not pausing to look into the eyes of anyone else as I went and ran straight out into the blinding rain. It pounded my skin like a hammer, the drops were so big, but I fought through the beating in order to wipe my eyes and scan the parking lot. His motorcycle sat untouched, soaked in its spot, and the roar of the rain overwhelmed the rest of my senses.

I looked first to my right and then to my left, but the driving sheets of water almost made me miss him.

White material clung to his chest like a survivor to a life raft, and the unruly scraps of his ugly hair clung to the sides of his face like a wet mop.

Barefoot and broken, I moved my feet toward him, one in front of the other until there was no holding back my run.

His head lifted at the last second as my body crashed into his and my desperate hands grabbed at the side of his face.

Water streamed over the lines of his cheeks like river rocks, and vitality surged into his eyes as vibrantly as a flash of lightning.

My lips attacked his, eating at their softness and rushing to cover the entirety of each surface. He tasted like sin and chocolate and the forbidden dream of a stronger-minded woman.

I lived inside that dream, savoring the feel of his hands as they grasped at my hips and molded my soaked body to his. His mouth grappled with mine until I finally ceded control, and for the first time in my life, I moved in the same direction.

Letting him lead the moment and the kiss, I blocked out the sound of the rain and instead listened to the pound of his honest heart.

One second bled into the next, the threat of discovery only heightening my passion and driving me to grab at his shoulders and chest with ferocity and impatience. He maneuvered me by lifting me up and swinging my bare legs around his hips. I felt him move, but focused on the feel of his advancing lips. Each step only strengthened his fervor, and leached directly into me through the connection of our mouths.

My back hit the side of the building after he rounded the corner out of view, and even if I wasn't cognizant of it in that exact moment, I knew I appreciated his proclivity for discretion.

"Callie—" he gasped through a breath, moving his mouth from mine to my jaw and working it to the line of my neck.

I couldn't pull him close enough fast enough.

It felt like I'd been waiting forever.

Like this was as natural as breathing.

And, swaddled by the protection of the rain and a frozen moment in time, I allowed myself to savor it.

To squeeze the grip of my legs tighter and pull his body closer to mine.

Our wet clothes stuck to one another, and my leotard and what was left of his t-shirt left little to the imagination.

But I wanted what little there was.

I pulled at the hem of his shirt as he kissed from my collarbone up my neck and back again, sinking my fingers into the skin above the waistband of his pants and scratching.

He groaned into my mouth, and I moaned into his as we worked together toward the thing I found myself wanting more than anything in that moment—

CHAPTER TEN

Nik

Connection.

I wanted one with her almost more than I wanted my next breath, but I had no intention of taking it there pressed up against the cool metal of her family's gym. Not in the rain, not in the sun, and not within five miles of her peers.

We'd already been gone long enough that someone should have noticed, but I guess the rain had kept them from actually looking.

"Callie—" I called, prying my lips from hers and trying to move her hands *away* from the growing bulge in my pants.

I know. It sounded crazy to me too.

"Nik," she cooed back, still lost in the moment. I took the opportunity to pull back and look at her, covered in water and flushed from her nose to her ears and all the way down her exposed chest.

Her eyes were closed, and a droplet of water clung to the long, curled line of her lashes. Stretching to reach me, her lips parted and

81

pursed just slightly, and her hips shifted even closer to mine.

The skin of her thighs felt smooth and creamy, the now wet chalk forming a thin film of paste that made my hands harder to move.

I didn't mind, the feeling of my hands attached to her in a more powerful way than normal only deepened the need in my gut.

Her eyes opened as a result of my lull and looked questioningly into mine. Security fled and nerves started to encroach, her body language changing minutely in preparation for rejection. She thought this was it, the definition of catch and release.

Before she could retreat, I flexed the fingers of one hand deeper into one thigh and moved the other to cup the side of her face. My fingers mingled with the wet, straggling hairs of her ponytail that fell around the sides, and my thumb sought the supple corner of her lips.

I forced it up when it wanted to curve down and reassured her with actions as well as words.

"I'm in this, Cal. I'm not backing out, I'm not running away, and I'm not giving it up. I don't know what it is about you, but I couldn't forget this happened if I tried."

I'd been shocked as shit when her lips first met mine and momentarily mystified that my life had taken a path that somehow ended in this moment—fully enthralled mentally and physically with an athlete I'd been charged to coach and mentor—but at the feel of her and I together all of it faded away. The only thing left was awareness. A distinct recognition that something existed between us that neither one of us could manage to deny.

She seemed surprised that I could read her so well, but with me she'd always been a crystal clear page. No smudges to impede the context or fancy emotional language to get caught up in. Just smooth, simple prose that read true to her every emotion.

If other people had trouble reading her, they weren't very good at context clues.

"But we can't do this *here* any more than you can admit that I'm right."

"Hey!"

I smiled at the return of her fire. Anger or passion, it didn't matter to me. Just as long as it burned, I'd tend to it with care. Poke and nudge and rearrange when necessary. And any time she started to die out, I'd just add more fuel to the pile.

"How many people watched you leave?"

"Oh my God," she squeaked, the realization of consequences and aftermath slapping her on the cheek and leaving it red with embarrassment. "I can't go back in there. Not like this ..."

She looked down at herself, the sopping material of her leotard, her hair mussed from the rain and my hands, and the paste-y chalk evidence of my touch plastered over nearly every inappropriate surface illustrating her point. "Not after leaving like that."

"We don't have to go back in," I assured her, running my thumb from her lips to her ear and back again just because I could. Just because she wasn't stopping me from touching her, wasn't fighting me on the validity of what had happened.

I took a moment to soak it in and tried to telegraph the feeling it evoked in me right back to her.

"But we can't stay here."

"You don't have to go home, but you can't stay here? Are we at a bar?" Her head thunked back into the metal of the building behind her. "That'd be handy actually. I could use a drink."

"Callie," I called, asking for attention by pulling her face back toward mine with two soft fingers at her chin. "This is big. I get it, I feel it, and I'm just as confused about how it happened as you are. But I need you to calm down ... and focus. We cannot stay here right now. Especially not, as much as I enjoy it, with your sexy as fuck bare legs wrapped around my waist and my hard dick crushing you into the building."

"Crushing me?" she teased with a tilt of her head. "You sure think a lot about your—"

"Cal!"

"Okay! I get it! We need to leave." She rolled her eyes playfully. "Then take me somewhere for crying out loud."

Regretfully, I unwound her legs from me and set her bare feet on the ground, steadying her swaying body as it lurched toward me in unbalance. Her body's lingering physical reaction gave me some clue as to why her mental realization of our scenario was delayed as well.

She was still turned on and tuned up on adrenaline, and apparently, lust made her frolicsome.

Fuck me.

I didn't know if she always reacted this way or if it was the intensity and unexpected nature of the moment, but I had absolutely no desire to waste it. I wanted to get her somewhere else, somewhere where I could work her back up to that reaction again, and I wanted to do it quickly.

I grabbed her hand and ran, pulling her behind me into the more brutal rain of the open parking lot. Her hand clenched tightly in mine when a gust of wind drove the rain like horizontal spikes.

The pound of her bare feet on the pavement behind me sounded like a rhythm, each step jolting through my chest and confirming the unbelievable fact that we were here. That she had followed me from the gym, that she'd been the one to kiss me.

All of it felt like an imaginary whirlwind. Her car only feet away, I dropped her hand in preparation and rounded the hood, hoping to everything holy that she kept her keys in the car rather than her bag in the gym. If not, we'd have to take the motorcycle, and besides the rain, I didn't like the idea of her riding with so much unprotected skin exposed.

"Keys?" I called over the hood, just as she opened the passenger door.

She nodded with knowing, pointing inside the car and sinking into the seat and out of the rain.

I yanked my door open and threw one leg in, but looked up as I did.

Right into the eyes of Frank Nickleson.

Hands on his hips, he stood stagnant on the other side of the glass door, keen and curious eyes on me and the very familiar car I was waiting to sink into.

Panic very nearly jolted my body—for Callie rather than myself—but I fought it, instead giving him a resolute, confident nod with an open ended meaning.

He could contemplate his own clues, paint his own picture, and draw his own conclusions.

But I'd planted a seed of doubt with one simple gesture.

Guilty men, fraught with wrongdoing and wicked intentions, rarely looked their jury directly in the eye.

And after trusting me to guide his daughter professionally, no matter the age of consent and lack of dissent between hers and my own, Frank Nickleson would very much see me as a guilty man if he knew the details of my intentions for my relationship with her.

As I slid into the car, desperate to hold on to the fun, free-loving woman unlocked by a kiss, I decided not to tell Callie about her father's watchful eye. Not if she hadn't noticed it on her own.

Mischief and happiness sparkled in her eyes as she turned to me. "Where are we going?"

"My apartment," I decided and decreed at once, wanting the privacy and freedom to talk to her how I wanted, touch her how I wanted, and open up the next chapter of her beautifully written book.

All of the things she'd kept locked away for the last few weeks lingered on the surface, and I was eager to scrape as many of them up as I could before they disappeared.

A shiver ran through her body as she opened the console between us, grabbed the keys from inside, and handed them to me with an electric brush of her hand.

"Cold?" I asked as I started the engine, ignoring the man that still stood in front of us and focusing on her.

"A little," she admitted, turning on the heat and pointing the vent until air directly bathed her skin.

I wanted to pull her into my arms, warm her with the heat of my own body and the comfort of my arms, but I knew it wasn't a good idea.

"I'm sorry. It won't take long to get there," I said instead, watching as her brows scrunched slightly together before turning away and putting the car into gear.

Hurt feelings and unmet expectations would have to wait.

I turned left out of the parking lot and drove toward the center of town. Past the McDonald's where we'd shared greasy chicken nuggets, a Quarter Pounder, and nervously aggressive conversation, through Main Street, and to the apartment complex on the other side that housed my home.

I missed the home I shared with my parents throughout my childhood, but not because of the house. I missed the laughter of my mother and the playful antics by my father that caused it. I missed the loving acceptance they provided me through all of my decisions, the support they gave to my athletic career, and their ability to balance that with a life devoid of pressure.

I didn't think Callie had that—an unconditional support system.

I wanted to be that for her.

As I pulled into the spot directly in front of my unit, Callie's voice cracked with nerves. The fog of lust and passion had worn off, and reality had set in. "What are we doing, Nik?"

I turned to her fully, put a hand to her jaw, and leaned in until my lips just barely touched hers. She didn't pull back or protest, but the pulse in her neck throbbed violently.

"What we've wanted to do since the first night we met." When the words were finished, the movement fully formed against her lips, I added pressure, settling my mouth against hers and sealing the statement with a kiss.

She kissed me back slowly, the taste of cinnamon and heat working its way into my mouth along with her tongue as she gave into the moment and allowed herself the freedom from her mind.

I never wanted it to end, but I also wanted more than stolen kisses and unsure rendezvous.

And that kind of more was only founded on *more*. More communication, more understanding, and more respect.

Breaking the kiss slowly, I let my hand linger on her cheek, feeling it heat with both embarrassment and something else as her eyes met mine.

"Let's go inside, okay?" I asked softly.

"Yeah," she agreed with a nod, staring into my eyes for a beat longer and then turning to open her door. I followed suit, rounding the hood and walking beside her to ensure she didn't step on something that would hurt either of her bare feet.

My bag inconveniently still in my bike at the gym, I reached around the side of my door, behind the bush and pulled the hidden key out of its box before shoving it in the lock and opening the door.

With an extended arm, I suggested she go first, flipping on the switch for the light in the hall as I stepped in behind her.

"Just down and to your right," I suggested, guiding her to the living room.

When she got to the opening, she hesitated.

Her eyes found mine as she asked, "Do you think I could take a quick shower? I'm sticky from the chalk and the rain kind of—"

"Of course." I cut her off before hearing the rest. It didn't matter why, other than meaning it needed rectifying.

"Come on," I said. My hand fit directly in the slight hollow of her lower back, and her steps, though her legs were much shorter than mine, matched me beat for beat.

I reached around the wall in order to flick on the light switch in the bathroom, pushing the door out of the way and standing back to let her enter. "There are towels under the sink, shampoo and stuff in the shower. Sorry if it smells like guy, but—" I hollowed my cheeks in jest, "that's kind of how I like to smell."

She smiled slightly and stepped into the space, but as I turned to leave she stopped me with a hand to my shoulder.

"Is this how it's gonna be from now on?"

"How do you mean?"

"I don't know. Awkward. Overly nice. Tiptoeing around one another?" she offered.

I only hid part of my smile. "For right now? Yeah, probably," I admitted. "See, I'm a little skittish about running you off and you're trying your best to convince me you can be something other than crabby."

"Hey!"

I released the rest of my smile, letting it soar all the way to the tops of my cheeks and pull at the corners of my eyes.

And then I winked. "Don't worry, though. Something tells me it won't last."

Her shoulders relaxed at the same pace as her face, draining her of tension and filling its void with understanding.

She'd still give me a hard time, and I was more than happy to give one back. There would never be a time when we didn't yell, and no matter how right I was, she'd still fight me on admitting it.

But we'd get to fool around a little.

I, personally, felt like it couldn't get much better than that.

"Go shower," I instructed. "I'll get you some clothes to put on."

"Thanks," she replied. Both of us knew she didn't just mean for the clothes.

My bedroom just down the hall, I got a pair of shorts, boxers, and a t-shirt out of my dresser fairly quickly and headed back for the bathroom.

The water was on, but I knocked to make sure she was inside and not standing naked in the middle of the bathroom. It wasn't that I didn't want her to be that way or didn't want to see it, but I had a feeling she felt everything I was feeling times a million.

And to me, the whole day felt—

CHAPTER ELEVEN

Callie

Surreal.

Before Nik had shown up a little over three weeks ago, I would have sworn up and down that unicorns shitting rainbows and giant cars made of candy were a more realistic possibility than me getting mixed up in some pseudo-forbidden romance with anyone, let alone my new coach.

Add in the fact that I knew I'd have to face questions about my behavior that day at some point—I lived with my parents for shit's sake—and my head was reeling.

Spinning and spiraling to figure out the ups and the downs and how to make it all order itself into something that made sense. Something that fit in with the person I thought I was or proved irrefutably that I'd been wrong all along. I couldn't settle on either scenario, my world stuck in the limbo in between. I'd never been in between two places before.

At least, it didn't seem like it. I knew I had been, the impossibility of getting from one place to the other without passing through the area in between crystal cut. But I usually made moves with precision, a straight line of least resistance and notably lacking in traffic.

In some ways, I hadn't traveled much at all, sticking to my comfort zone even if I pushed at my levels of adaptability within it. I'd never felt like I was truly losing something that I desperately wanted to gain.

And that fact left me somewhat inexperienced emotionally in addition to physically.

The smell of Nik's shampoo had me nearly coming out of my skin as I massaged it into my hair, the memory of its scent lodged in my brain from the moment I'd put my eager searching hands into his hair. The wet from the rain revived the scent as we'd kissed, bleeding it into the air like a slow release valve for the air on your tires.

A knock sounded on the door.

"Yeah?"

It cracked open slowly, a low-pitched squeal just barely emanating from poorly oiled hinges.

"I'll just leave the clothes here on the counter," Nik said without preamble or waiting for a reply. The door shut behind him with a click, and my head followed it by sinking into my hands.

I had to laugh to myself as I stood there under the warm water, bathed in the lingering awkwardness of his delivery.

Nervousness seeped off of his normally confident figure in the way he moved and spoke and looked at me. He said all of the right words, plugged all of the right holes, and answered all of the right questions, but he felt just as lost as me.

And the beauty of that was it made me feel a little less lost after all.

It was a spin on the old, "Not all those who wander are lost."

For me, *for us*, I couldn't help but feel that those who wander aimlessly together, aren't, in fact, aimless at all.

When the last of the shampoo rinsed from my hair and the last of the soap slipped from my body, I turned off the water and stepped out.

His towel was fluffy and new, and its scent suggested a fresh wash.

I'd noticed briefly on the way in that everything seemed tidy and thoughtfully placed too. I wasn't sure if this was an insight into his personality or if he just hadn't spent enough time here to mess it up, but I logged the information and stored it for later, just in case.

His clothes were baggy, but not by too much, the muscle tone of his athletic body more lean that meaty.

I finger combed the strands of my hair and left them loose, took one last look in the mirror and deep breath in my lungs, and stepped out into the quiet darkness of the hallway.

The utter silence was disconcerting, but I figured with the riotous mess my nerves were, there could be a full blown concert taking place in his apartment and I still wouldn't have felt completely at ease.

A small beacon of light shone from the living room, so I padded along the dark, berber carpet to the opening he'd shown me before and peeked inside. I didn't know quite what to expect from any of it. From him, from our intimate encounter, or if it would directly lead into more.

I felt torn, both wanting to pick up where we left off and anxiously unready at the same time. When I'd stormed out of the gym, I'd been lost in myself and my mind and the lingering effects of him. Now, fresh from my shower, I'd scrubbed some of my boldness away, shining the surface to a cautiously inhibited clean.

"Hey," he greeted me immediately from his spot on the couch, dry clothes replacing his previously soaked ones.

"Hey," I waved back, unsure of where we were supposed to go

from here.

I felt comfortable in his apartment, as much as I could under the circumstances, and I trusted him not to push me, but my experience in all things adult was limited.

I'd lived a very tunneled life, the traffic of my intentions flowing in one very distinct direction—Olympic greatness. That left little time for anything else, romantic or otherwise.

Now that I wanted it, I didn't know how to take it.

"You look like a frightened puppy," he called out, making my contemplative eyes jerk to his.

Mine narrowed slightly in mildly affronted reaction. "You don't look exactly at ease yourself," I argued.

Laughter rolled from deep in his chest, up the column of his throat, and out of his appealing mouth, letting out the breath we'd both been holding in one swift moment.

"You're right."

I walked over to him as he spoke and sat down on the couch across from him. His hand automatically sought mine, his fingers pushing through mine and settling into a hold that felt strangely like home.

"Let's break the ice," he suggested. "We'll each admit something embarrassing to each other. Something you haven't told anyone else and have tried your best to forget yourself."

"Oh, yeah," I grumbled, horrified. "That sounds like a great idea."

He laughed at my obvious sarcasm and squeezed my hand, pulling the pair of them until the back of his entwined hand rested on his thigh. I watched as it went but pried my eyes free when he spoke again.

"It won't be that bad. I'll go first." He took a deep breath and exhaled, but when I expected him to start his confession, he stalled a little more instead. "Just remember that this exercise is meant to endear me to you. If I find out you're selling my secrets on the internet,

I'll be pissed."

"No selling your embarrassing tales on the internet. Got it." He nodded, but I held up a finger to slow him. "*Unless*, I stand to gain a fortune weighty enough to sustain independent wealth."

One corner of his mouth hitched up.

"If they're willing to pay that much, I'll probably tell," I teased through a face scrunch and a shrug.

"Deal," he agreed good-naturedly, his whole being alight with humor and goodness.

I'd never considered the kind of man I wanted enough to know what qualities that included ahead of time.

The more I spent time with him, though, the more that list of non-existent qualities looked like him.

Patient. Forgiving. Unflappably rational.

Engaged in me and life and everything around him.

He actually *spoke* with his eyes, crinkling the corners and narrowing them just enough to make me notice when he was choosing his words carefully. They widened infinitesimally when he was working harder to make me agree with his point or when he really wanted me to listen. And they were just as expressive when he was listening to me. They emoted his every feeling and absorbed each accompanying one of mine.

I'd been noticing all along, but forcing myself to forget.

I most certainly wasn't forgetting right then.

"Okay," he said, getting himself ready to admit one of his best kept secrets. "Embarrassing. God, yeah, this fits the bill." He paused again. "Who's idea was this again?"

I laughed. "Yours."

He nodded his resignation. "Right. Okay, so. I was fourteen, right?"

"I imagine you were at one time, yes," I goaded.

He shook his head in amusement. "Well, you know what fourteen is like for guys—"

I raised my brows.

He chuckled and pushed his hair back out of his eyes in discomfort. "Okay, right, I guess you don't." He bit his bottom lip and considered his words carefully. "It's a temperamental time for a young man—hormonally."

I couldn't help the stupid smile from forming on my face and sticking, both corners of my mouth secured indefinitely to the corners of my eyes.

"Jennifer Joffries was the hottest gymnast in my gym, all hips and overdeveloped breasts and long ass legs."

I narrowed my eyes and glanced down, my lack of boobs standing out like a neon sign between us.

He shook his head, pushed more hair out of his face with his free hand.

Where was his hat? Oh. Probably in his motorcycle. At the gym.

"No, see, I was fourteen. I mentioned that, right?"

"A time or two."

"And Jennifer started gymnastics after puberty, so her growth wasn't stunted like the rest of the girls."

"Still not sure I'm liking this."

"Okay, okay," he rushed. "You don't realize this, but at fourteen, for guys, boobs are all that matter. At twenty-eight, I've got an entirely different favorite part."

I felt the flush sweep through me from face to feet.

Point taken.

He chuckled at my easy embarrassment and grabbed onto my other hand to hold it too. Shin to shin, each of us had one leg tucked up on the couch and the other foot on the floor, both hands securely in each others' hold. I was pretty sure it was one of the best forms of contact I'd ever felt.

"One day after practice, I finally got up the nerve to talk to her,

95

and we ended up making out in the locker room. It was great."

I couldn't help but laugh at his boyish frankness.

"That is until I got a little overly worked up, and she pointed it out to the entirety of the gym, my parents included."

"Ouch! Jennifer sounds like a total bitch."

"Nah," he denied. "Just fourteen and female."

I shook my head at his generalization and bumped him in the inner thigh with the back of our hands. He scrambled to defend against a potential blow to the jewels.

"Well, that was fun," I redirected, hoping he'd move on and let me off the hook. No such luck.

"Nuh uh uh. It's your turn. Come on, Cal. Feed my soul. Give me some redemption. Prove to me that I'm not alone," he fake pleaded, widening his eyes comically and making it impossible to resist.

The only thing I could think of was the one thing I didn't want to say, but eager to get it over with, I blurted it all out at once anyway. "I lost my virginity to a guy who used to do gymnastics at the gym right after my first Olympics. I thought he really liked me, but he really just wanted to say that he'd been with the un-fuckable. And to make matters worse it happened in the basement of a high school house party with "Touch My Body" by Mariah Carey playing in the background. To this day, I skeeve out anytime I see her on TV."

Across from me, Nik sat frozen, his body a statue and his face a bland mask of discomfort.

"You're not laughing," I pointed out.

He scoffed. "Because it isn't fucking funny. Why is that women always think fucked up situations like that are embarrassing for them? That fucking asshole douche of a kid should be ashamed of himself. Not you."

"I—"

"I bet he didn't even give you an orgasm."

The air left my lungs in such a hurry, I nearly choked.

Unable to speak, I settled for a shake of my head.

"What a fucking cocksucker."

"Nik—"

"The next guy treated you right, right?"

At this point, the conversation had turned laughable, so I didn't even pause before my admission. "What next guy?"

In one fast tug he had me up off the couch and headed down the hall.

"What are you doing?"

He stopped so fast, I nearly ran into him, looking directly at me and barking his answer.

"Treating you goddamn right."

My face jerked back and warmed as his words washed over me.

"The romance is ripe," I poked in jest as he started speed walking again and pulled me directly into his bedroom and onto the bed.

The gray cotton cover felt soft under my thighs as his baggy loaner shorts road up, but the sound of his gravelly voice roughened the moment just enough. "Right now isn't about romance. It's about pleasure and lust and teaching you the bare minimum you should ever settle for physically."

I gulped an angry swallow down my tightening throat and curled into the growing ache in my abdomen. His words felt alive in a way that caressed each and every one of my senses.

His face pushed closer to mine.

"And I can guarantee when it comes to the minimum for you, there's nothing mini about it."

His earnest eyes met mine deliberately, and with the way he said the words, the way his eyes spoke as he did, there wasn't a thing in the world that could convince me that when Nik said those words to me, there was a single one that didn't breathe romance.

"*Nik.*"

"Let me make you feel good, Cal. Just you tonight." His body trapped mine, pushing me gently back onto the bed until he hovered right above me, his lips inches from mine and affection in his crystal blue eyes. He smoothed the still damp hair from my face and kissed the skin he uncovered by doing it. Slowly, deliberately, worshipping. "Just you coming apart in my arms and you trusting me to be the one to make it happen."

Goosebumps emblazoned my arms like a finely crafted textile as his words and movements swept over me. My eyes closed of their own accord.

Tender fingers pried the hem of his baggy t-shirt away from my body languidly, skimming the skin as they went and making my hips sink into the bed even further. Air tunneled under my back as it arched slightly, the feeling of his skin on mine even more electrifying without the aid of sight.

His lips touched each eyelid individually. I felt his breath caress my face when he spoke in a need-roughened whisper. "Trust me to make you feel good, Callie."

"I do," I admitted easily because I did. I didn't know what that meant precisely or how he intended to achieve it, but I knew he'd do his best to take care of me.

Wide hands slid up the smooth muscle of my belly, and his lips moved slowly from the curve of my ear to my collarbone. The neck of my shirt impeded his progress.

Asking silent permission, he lifted and tugged at it, bringing it to the line just beneath my bare breasts and stopping. The material bunched and billowed, and the halt in progress made me itchy with need.

Knowing he wouldn't go any further without my okay, I lifted my arms and granted him the room he needed to remove the barrier of cotton.

I opened my eyes when it cleared my face so I could watch his as he took in all of my exposed skin.

Eager and unfocused his eyes ate up every square inch of surface area, dilating at the sight of my chest. There wasn't much there to see as far as I was concerned, but he didn't look like a man unfulfilled. He looked like a man starved for the exact meal I was offering.

Lowering his head slowly, he rested his lips in the hollow of my throat and breathed. I could feel them move against my skin like a hundred tiny kisses as he spoke. "You're beautiful, Calia."

My full name felt strange and wonderful at once. I expected him to move quickly, but he didn't. Instead he rested there for long moments breathing along with the rhythm moving in and out of my own throat. But I didn't feel awkward in the least.

"Nikolai," I called back, testing out the feel of his full name on my lips and producing a smile on his. They dragged along my skin as they curved, leaving a damp trail and accompanying chill in their wake.

Tweaking my ear briefly with his nose, his hands trailed up the lean line of my sides and settled on the span of my rib cage. My upper body was bigger in base than my middle and my thighs held equally disproportional mass. That was the body of a gymnast.

Traveling lips ghosted the line of my neck and down my chest, zeroing in on my nipple and sucking before I had time to prepare. Sparks flew in a direct line from there to the ache between my legs and deepened it. I expected relief in his pursuits but didn't find it, instead feeling myself build higher and higher into a frenzy with each thoughtful lave of his tongue.

His fingers toyed at the waistband of my shorts playfully before diving underneath to stroke the skin. I found myself wanting his hand to travel further, wanting his fingers to toy with me rather than the waistband. I didn't have a ton of experience, and part of that had always ashamed me. It had always felt like a disadvantage to make it to twenty-six years old with only one crappy sexual experience to count, but it didn't feel that way anymore.

This man and place were right. I wasn't fully convinced about the timing, but the more he did and the closer he got to my sex, the more I came around to that thinking.

His lips came back to mine at the exact moment his fingers found my clit, and the combination made me feel like I'd go blind.

Stars and blackness alternated behind my lids at random, and the caress of his tongue on mine made the time needed comically short.

With a moan I hadn't known was possible, I came apart just as one of his long fingers settled inside me. It didn't feel invasive or foreign. It felt welcome.

And my body reacted accordingly. Sucking and milking it in an effort to pull it deeper, my sex sought to keep his finger there, probably forever if possible, and clenched at the girth of it with release. Fire burned through my body and all voluntary function ceased to exist. Only Nik and my pleasure could change the way I acted in that moment.

"God, Cal," he breathed into the skin at my neck, tucking his face there and inhaling my scent. His body shook on top of mine and his hand made no effort to retreat.

When my hands found the will to move again, I put them to his back, scooting his t-shirt up and smoothing them over his slick skin in an effort to get closer.

I cringed at the rough and ragged feel of my touch, immediately withdrawing my hands in embarrassment.

He noticed the retreat and made an accompanying one of his own, but only as to position himself so he could see my face.

"What's wrong?"

"Nothing."

"Callie," he protested, putting one gentle finger to the curve of my chin.

"Something changed. What is it? Did I make you uncomfortable—" he surveyed with worry, breaking me nearly immediately with guilt.

"No. Nik, it's not that. I ... that was wonderful." I closed my eyes tight against the shame before opening them to my admission at once. "It's just my hands."

"Your hands?"

I searched for the words to explain, and he waited patiently until they formed. "I've been fighting for this. Fighting and clawing and scratching for nearly my entire life."

He nodded along, confirming that he'd followed me along my nonsensical path from hands to gymnastics. The best part was that he wasn't just appeasing me. It seemed to make sense to him too. I lifted one hand in front of our faces and studied it.

"And sometimes I feel like all I have to show for it are these battered hands."

"Your hands aren't battered," he denied in a whisper.

"They're not?"

He shook his head and reached out to rub his thumb over the brutalized skin of my rips.

"They're beautiful." His eyes left the motion of this caress and lifted to meet mine. "Mental and physical toughness. Determination. Dedication. Hard work. Someone I *want* to *know*. Those are the things your hands say to me."

Drugged on the high of my night with Nik, I didn't think about what would be waiting for me at home after I dropped him back at the gym to get his motorcycle, gave him one last kiss, and headed there.

I moved with the invincible mindset of a teenager for the first time, and it had only taken me seven extra years to get there.

The time was late but not obscene at a quarter past ten, and the lights were largely extinguished on the interior of our house as I pulled in the driveway.

I guess that's why the harsh sound of my father's voice calling out to me as I walked in the door nearly sent me into cardiac arrest.

"Where've you been, Calia?"

The question itself was preposterous for a twenty-six year old woman to have to answer without protest, but I understood the concept of respect. I'd stormed out of the gym without thought or explanation early that day—something that was highly unlike me—and disappeared without a reachable trace for nearly the rest of the day. He had a right to ask as a concerned loved one whether I thought he was in the position to be fatherly or not.

I tried for vague, knowing I absolutely couldn't go with the truth. "I just needed to clear my head."

His eyes narrowed. "What's going on with Nik?"

My chest seized and I nearly ingested my tongue. A couple of forced, rough swallows made it possible to speak again.

"We fought," I admitted, largely leaving out the details and hoping he'd take it at face value.

He shook his head in exasperation. "What else is new?"

"I apologized."

Understatement.

"Well, that's definitely different."

I fought the instinct to roll my eyes. Now was not the time to egg my father on and instigate more questions than necessary. Now was the time to contain the blast and get out with minimal damage.

"I drove him home since he's only got the motorcycle and the rain was so bad." I gestured gallantly outside for added effect. Cleared my throat. "I think one of his friends was going to run him back later to get his motorcycle or something. Then I just drove around for a while to visualize my routines and get back in the right mindset."

Unbelievably, he nodded with approval, and I sighed a huge

breath of relief. I hadn't been too bad at lying for not having tried my hand at it much in the past. I wasn't sure that was a good thing, but tonight, I was thankful. I'd sell my soul to just about any devil to keep my night with Nik, and this was a small price to pay comparatively.

Tonight had been happiness, fulfillment, and fantasy.

Tonight had been—

CHAPTER TWELVE

Nik

Harmony.

I could hear it, I could feel it, we *were* it today. As poorly as yesterday had gone in the gym, today had gone equally, but well. The intensity and passion were largely the same, but the vibe behind them was shockingly positive.

I'd half expected her to retreat into her shell after last night, but instead she shone from the inside out.

It was one of the best things I'd ever seen.

Her toes pointed with extra flex and her arms extended even taller over the top of her head. Her eyes were shiny with amusement, and the curve of her lips made her that much more enjoyable to watch.

Having just finished the second tumbling pass in her floor routine—a tumbling pass in which she very much pushed all the way through her toes and into the floor like an explosion—she gave me a sly look of mischief and mystery that had my heart beating faster.

She was flirting with me as she worked, using each movement to remind me of an intimate encounter that had been beyond all of my wildest dreams. She'd been sensational last night, preening and succumbing to all of my ministrations without inhibition. Her body moved with just as much fluidity now, dancing from one skill to the next with precision and beauty that vibrated out from her body and encompassed the large room.

I could feel the eyes of everyone else, pulled in to her routine by her talent alone. I watched for that and more.

Careful to keep my leering to a fairly discreet minimum, I harnessed my focus and straightened my coaching hat. There was a time to watch her body, her reactions to my touch, and the way her breath left her mouth in her most pleasure filled moments.

This wasn't it.

The music reached a crescendo and struck the last note just as she struck her final pose—one hand to her chest and the other to the ceiling, her head thrown back in a flourish of brilliance. She held it briefly before coming directly to me with a smile on her face.

"Well?" she prompted on gloat, knowing she'd been on point, that her execution had been what I'd been demanding of her the whole time.

After weeks of criticism she wanted to feel my praise rain down over her to the point that she could roll around in it like a pig in mud.

"You were peacocking," I accused, catching her off guard.

"Peacocking?" she questioned, pulling the band of her ponytail looser, adjusting the fit with a shake, and then pulling it tight again.

"Yep," I confirmed with a wag of my brows and a chuckle. "Showing off your feathers in an illustrious display of dominance and seduction. Reeling me in with your beauty with each turn and presentation."

She thought about it for two beats before laughing. "Well,

damn. That sounds like exactly what I was doing." She shrugged and stretched the line of her face with acceptance. "Did it work?"

I shook my head in false denial and gave her my most meaningful eyes. "Like you wouldn't believe."

She wiped a hand down each arm and followed it up with a shove to my shoulder. "Well, feel free to stroke my feathers and call me Peacock, baby."

A loud bark of laughter burst from my mouth unexpectedly and pulled the attention of several surrounding girls. I saw it as the perfect opportunity to move Callie's social issues in the right direction.

I didn't want to change her. But she wanted the change herself. It was in the way she talked about her place in the gym, the loneliness she felt in her isolation.

Callie was a warm, kind-hearted, often funny woman all on her own. I just had to give her the opportunity to realize I wasn't the only one who saw it.

"Hey, girls!" I greeted with a lift of my hand.

"Hey, Coach Nik!" they yelled back enthusiastically.

Callie's mouth moved in a silent mock. "Coach Nik?"

"Yep, that's right," I confirmed before instructing, "Say hi."

"Say hi?"

"To the girls. Come on, do it before it's weird," I urged in a whisper.

Confused, she turned back toward the girls stiffly but followed direction. "Hi, girls," she greeted with a wave.

All of them immediately fluttered and tittered with excitement.

"She said hi!"

"Oh my God!"

"Calia Nickleson knows who we are!"

All at once and on top of one another they giggled and spewed their excitement through harsh whispers.

Finally, they got it together, reciting, "Hi, Calia!" in enthusiastic unison.

Callie turned back to me with wide-eyed shock.

I couldn't help but gloat a little. "Enlightening, huh?"

She agreed, but admitting that to me just wasn't her style. "Proud of yourself, are you?"

"You bet your sweet ass," I agreed with a wink and a smile.

She rolled her eyes as I plotted my next strategic move in our game of verbal chess.

"You have to admit that I'm good. I mean, come on. Before I got here, those girls hated you, right? Resented you for your successes and everything that meant about you?"

She narrowed her eyes in suspicion.

"You told me that yourself." I pointed at her and then brought the palm of my hand flat against my chest. "So, yeah, I'm proud of myself for turning it around."

"You are not responsible for turning it around," she argued just because she could. Her ponytail whipped in denial. "What did you do? Hang out in the locker room and talk me up?"

"No." I chewed softly at the bottom half of my lips to keep my grin from growing out of control.

"Exactly."

"Exactly what?"

Exasperated, she snapped, "You didn't fix it!"

"Right you are," I agreed, momentarily throwing her off and making her chest heave back slightly. "Because there was never anything to fix but your crusty exterior. You said hi and those girls practically threw up all over themselves to say it back."

One corner of her mouth curled up in aggravated astonishment.

"Though," I said with a lift of one finger, "I *am* the one who's helped revive you from your grumpy ways. And forced you to say hello. So, really, I *did* fix it."

She shook her head and scrunched her nose with ill-concealed humor. "Just shut up and follow me to Vault."

I crossed my arms and hid a smile behind the cup of one hand. She turned in a huff, whipping the tail her long, tied back hair over her shoulder as she did.

"Yes, ma'am," I called to her back, inconspicuously watching her butt sway side to side as she walked in front of me.

"Ew." Her head jerked around to look at me. "Don't call me ma'am. That's creepy."

"How about I call you Peacock?" I offered magnanimously.

"Um, no." She squinted further in disgust. "Pea, maybe. You can keep the cock for yourself."

"I *have* the cock. I am the cock. I do not want to keep it to myself."

"What is it that's happened that all of a sudden makes me feel like you might be a sex offender?"

"Stop!" I choked out through a laugh, looking around cautiously since she hadn't bothered to manage her volume.

"Just do that whole coaching thing you're supposed to be doing."

"I can't coach you until you actually do something," I pointed out, leaning against the wall next to the vault and gesturing to the end of the runway.

"Always me having to do all the stuff," she grumbled good-naturedly as she retightened the lion's paws around her wrists.

"I tell you what," I offered with a gallant bow as I shoved away from the wall. "I'll set up your spring board for you."

She stuck out her tongue. "That's your job."

I nodded again, smiling as I did and wagging my brows. "And gymnastics is yours."

Her face was alight and alive, and I soaked it in, letting it feed my mind and body.

With one last shake, she turned and retreated, heading for the end of the runway and trusting me to set everything up to her liking.

We joked and jested like that for the rest of the day, and if I was honest, I hadn't even considered the fact that people were watching us and taking notice. That our normally aggressive banter had toned way down in aggression, and the way we looked at each other may as well have been a beacon for anyone looking to find an example of flirtation and affection.

I'd made certain not to touch her with my hands unless she legitimately needed a spot, but I didn't really have to.

The way I touched her with my eyes already said it all.

"You only wear purple. Why?" I asked as I sat across from her on the end of the rod floor, wrapping my ankles in layer after layer of tape in order to tumble.

"Ha," she mock-laughed looking down to the offending material and then away toward the other side of the empty gym. "I guess I'm just wearing my bruises on the outside."

"That's not it," I denied as I looked at the back of her head. She was lying, and she wasn't doing it well.

With a slow but unyielding turn, her eyes met mine. "How can you tell?"

"Because then you'd be in red," I said simply. Her face turned questioning, but she didn't say anything. By now, she knew I'd explain. I always did.

"You're insides are bloodied, not bruised."

"Geez," she groaned, mildly affronted.

I chuckled. "Come on, Cal. You know I like your bloody inner gore."

An agitated sigh left her mouth in staccato.

"Why do you really wear it?"

She shook her head and looked at a swirl in the material at her neck.

"It's stupid."

"So what if it is?" I asked.

Her arm reached out in order to shove me playfully until my back hit the floor. "Thanks. You're supposed to tell me that there's no way it's stupid."

I shrugged as I sat up, curling my abs and reaching for the tape for my fingers as I did. "Sorry. But it might be. And that's okay. You're allowed to do stuff for stupid reasons every once in a while. I don't think the fact that I look for the number nine in everything I do is logical or intelligent, but I still do it. Because I can."

"You look for the number nine in everything?"

"I just said I did," I confirmed with smile and tilt of my head.

"Do *I* look like a nine?"

"No."

"What? Not curved enough for you?" she teased, rolling her neck to the side and trying to connect it with her body.

"No," I replied. "You don't look like a nine," I paused, "because you're a ten."

Her eyes dilated both at the corniness of my assertion and the meaning behind it. She knew I said it not to get a reaction, but because I meant it.

Instead of lingering in the moment, she cleared her throat and went back to the original question.

"When I was younger, it was my favorite color. I wore it all the time because that's what twelve year olds do." She picked at the tight, short fiber of the foam carpet covering the rods. "But I loved gymnastics then. Looked forward to every day, every split, and each and every event. Last year when I started feeling like I'd lost my way, I don't know ... I guess I thought this might help."

My head cocked just slightly, wanting so badly to ask her more about her lack of love for the sport and why she kept doing it anyway.

But I didn't want to ruin what I knew was already a powerful admission on her part, so I forced myself to let it go.

Mostly.

"Did it?"

She laughed, the end of her ponytail swaying with the negative shake of her head. "Not even a little bit."

Her answer made my skin itch, so much so that my mental cortisone nearly wore off, but I fought it, keeping my question innocent rather than probing.

"But you're still doing it?" I queried after looking from her very purple leotard to her face and back again.

Her shoulders went up to her cute ears and back down. "I bought all new leotards and got rid of my old ones. They're all purple."

My laugh started as a low wheeze and turned into a barking cough as I fell back to horizontal on the floor.

She scooted toward me suddenly, covering my body with hers in annoyance.

"Don't laugh at me!"

"I couldn't stop if I tried, my little Pea," I admitted, happy and unable to hide it. There with her, in the gym alone at night with her simple admission floating through the air and mingling with all the leftover stirred up chalk of the day, I couldn't make myself want to be anywhere else.

She cringed at the nickname, but I found myself liking it. She was tiny in size, and yet, her presence was undeniable just like the pea under a certain princess' mattress.

The weight of her body settled on top of mine as her hands left the support of the ground and ventured into my hair. Pushing clumps and sweeping individual strands different directions, she played with the mop of it mindlessly for minutes as she did nothing else but stare directly into my eyes.

With bated breath, I did my best not to disturb her, desperate for her to keep it up.

Her nails unintentionally scratched at my scalp, and the motion of her actions tugged at the nerves at each sensitive root. It felt relaxing and personal and contentedly natural.

Just as she'd accused, while she worked, I watched.

The skin of her face was smooth and unflawed, and the lashes of her eyes curled with natural length and luster. She didn't wear much makeup from what I'd seen, instead sticking to striving for a subtle girl next door mystique.

She failed miserably.

Only because she couldn't hide the dimension of her irises or change the curve of her smile. Each cheek hooked all the way to her eyes when laughter robbed her face of seriousness, and raw power shone off of every muscular line of her perfectly honed body.

The way she moved when she was in her element only made it better.

"You're so pretty, Cal," I whispered, grabbing one of her hips with an open hand and settling the other palm on her warm back. "I don't think I've really told you that, but it's true. From the very first moment you glared at me, your eyes have been my undoing."

Speaking of the devils, they narrowed playfully at the use of the word 'glared'.

Still she said nothing as we lay there with our legs intertwined and touching, and as the silence stretched on, my curiosity started to over-ripen and bruise with worry.

"Callie?" I asked softly, wrapping my palm around the curve of her cheek.

Leaning forward, she touched her lips to mine, speaking with them there in the same way that I often did.

"Make love to me, Nik," she breathed on one soft exhale.

My eyes squeezed painfully shut before prying themselves open again.

Sweet Christ Almighty.

"Here?"

"Here," she nodded, resolute. "Right now."

"Cal—"

"I want to know how it's supposed to feel," she interrupted on a silky whisper, touching the very tip of her delicate nose to my large one.

I wasn't ashamed to admit a full body shiver made quick work of my six foot tall frame.

"God, Cal."

Pain from consideration splintered in my rational mind and indecision warred in my belly, but one team was fighting with an intensity that the other side had not one chance of matching.

I figured it had a hell of a lot to do with redirection of blood flow.

"I want to go on record as having said this is a bad idea."

Her eyes made an understated revolution before her lips settled softly atop mine once more. "You're hereby absolved of responsibility."

I shook my head in response, knowing I'd go head to head with any challenge whether I'd been the brain behind the idea or not. Especially one where I was *able* but completely *unwilling* to say no.

"Unnecessary," I murmured as I sealed her lips to mine, bringing a hand to the back of her exposed neck and pulling her even closer. "This is one action I find undeniably worth any and all consequences."

My only concern now was making it good for her. Making her feel comfortable and cared for and taking the super shitty reality of her first time and replacing it with memory much worthier of keeping.

She giggled as I rolled her, trapping her small body under mine and shifting my hardening hips directly into hers.

My hands went straight to her hips, digging and scraping and

113

trying to get under a hem that wasn't there.

"Of course you would have to be wearing the world's most impossible garment for achieving skin to skin contact," I grumbled as I kissed her neck, inhaling the smell of apples and citrus that seemed to seep from her skin. She'd been sweating and working all day, but she smelled as appealing as ever, and I was convinced that was another one of God's well-thought-out plans.

Not only was olfaction big in sensory memory, it was a scientific aphrodisiac, literally endearing you to people biologically matched to you.

Okay, I didn't have any actual research on the subject, but I could have sworn I'd seen an article about it at some point.

Callie's scent called to me, begging me to get closer, to burrow my way inside her skin and get as close as possible.

"There's skin everywhere," she disagreed through a laugh, her bare legs and arms curling around me with meaning.

And there was.

But it wasn't the skin that I wanted.

"You sure you want to do this here?" I asked, shaking my brain inside my head when it hinted at the fact that we (me, my brain, and my dick) didn't want to stop.

"Yeah," she confirmed quietly, nodding and slipping the strap of her leotard off of one smooth shoulder.

Knowing how tricky it was to get out of one of those damn things, I helped her slide her entire arm out and then repeated the process on the other side.

Languidly, fabric scraping softly over each nerve and eliciting goosebumps, I slid the rest of the leotard down. Past her hard-peaked chest, over the line of each rib, along the smooth ridges of her muscled abs, over the defined bones of her hips, and down the line of her toned legs.

Her turned on eyes followed me the whole way, meeting mine

when I was done with an intensity and security that astonished me.

The dichotomy between the trust she showed me and the skepticism she showed everyone else humbled me. I didn't know what I had done to deserve it.

"Why me?" I asked quietly, the desire to know outweighing everything and anything else in that moment.

Callie was, of course, confused. She hadn't been inside of my head to follow the same thought path I had.

"Why do you trust me?" I clarified, running my hands up her naked legs but focusing directly on her eyes.

They searched for the answer as she did, studying my face by touching on every part of it.

I knew it wasn't necessarily a fair or easy question. The complexity behind her reasoning would be hard enough to pinpoint, let alone condense into one, succinct statement.

It would be for me anyway.

"I don't know."

I nodded, knowing that I couldn't be disappointed at the lack of an answer for my difficult pop quiz, but she wasn't done.

"I guess it's because you've gone to great lengths to *see* me."

I smiled.

"And make sure I see you."

I leaned over, touching my lips to the skin of her abdomen and breathing her in. I felt satisfied. Justified in my intentions and actions.

Pulling my face up and away from her belly, she raised a brow in question.

"Why do you trust me?"

Just one corner of my mouth curved up, knowing I was going to bug the hell out of her.

"Same."

"Oh!" She smacked my shoulder and shoved at me as I started to laugh. "You cheater! A big, fat, cop-out of a cheater!"

"It's not my fault you took the good answer first," I remarked through my chuckle, appealing to her ego and accusation at the same time.

I trapped her hands as she swung at me, taking her arms by the wrists and pinning them to the ground above her head.

Laughter turned serious, and smiling eyes warmed to hot.

My hands slid into hers and our fingers interlaced as I settled my body on top of hers.

Air compressed and moved, vacating the narrowing space between us as I settled my lips onto hers. A sigh escaped through them and floated into mine as she opened herself to me.

My tongue worked in tandem with the slow grinding movement of my hips, caressing the tip of hers and soaking in the feel of it.

She felt incredible, all smooth skin and flexible limbs, and her legs came up to wrap around my waist.

I pulled back, though, not wanting to be trapped for fear that I wouldn't be able to make myself move again. And we still had too many layers of barrier between us.

Removing myself from her hold slowly and carefully, I sank my butt to my heels and pulled myself up to standing, shedding my shorts and underwear in one smooth movement.

Her eyes rounded from below me. The sight of me naked had either surprised or frightened her, but I was hoping for the first.

"You alright?" I asked.

She gulped and pushed up onto her elbows, thrusting her chest out further into my view without realizing. "Yeah, it's just ... you weren't naked and then all of a sudden you were."

"Hah!" I barked with humor. "That's usually how it works."

"No, I know. I was just expecting it to go ... slower." Her eyes were alight with mischief and fun and no longer held an air of fear, releasing me from worry and opening up the opportunity to taunt.

"You want me to do a striptease?"

"There's nothing left," she pointed out.

I pointed to one of my feet and offered, "I bet I could do a hell of a job making taking off my tape look sexy if you had your heart set on it."

Sudden realization froze her face, and she flopped back to the floor and let both arms flail down beside her. "Ahhh," she groaned.

"What?"

"I'll be more impressed if you can make something *appear*."

My eyebrows inched closer together.

"A condom," she specified, lifting her head to look at me.

Oh.

I laughed. "I have one in my bag."

"I want to ask why really badly right now," she said. "Instead, I'm just gonna be grateful."

"No illicit reason," I comforted with a smile and a shake of my head. "Just a routine. A strictly precautionary measure."

She bit her lip, satisfied with my answer, before jerking her head in the direction of my bag in suggestion.

I moved quickly and grabbed it, a small gasp of air breaking the silence from behind me as I bent over to dig through the contents.

When my fingers met foil, I ripped it immediately from the package and rolled it on.

Her eyes burned with want when I turned back around, and I wasted no time stalking her like prey. Each step felt like a mile, each second an hour. We'd spent so much time dancing around our attraction, and we hadn't acted any differently in this moment.

My hands went directly to her hips and hooked into the sides of her flesh colored underwear. Simultaneously, she curled her upper body off of the ground with nothing but the power of her abs and pulled her matching sports bra off.

Bared to my sight, her already peaked nipples hardened further, and my cock had no problem reciprocating.

It was the first time I'd seen her in all of her glory, so I took the desired time to appreciate her.

Golden skin blurred by a thin layer of chalk stretched from head to toe, and the pink of her lips, nipples, and sex stood out against it. Her chocolate eyes appeared darker, fading into the pupil with an indistinct delineation, and her soft brown hair fanned out from the band of her ponytail at the top of her head.

I reached over and removed the band, wanting to feel the movement of her loose hair as we came together.

She said nothing as I did it and nothing as I continued my perusal. Instead, she used the time to study me in equal detail.

One strip of perfectly neat, trimmed curls lined the top of her mound, and her clit and folds glistened with undisguised excitement.

I wanted to taste and touch her and eat at each and every one of the exposed inches of skin, but, with one read of my face and a shake of her head, she told me no.

"Inside, Nik," she instructed. "I'm tired of waiting."

Knowing she'd be plenty tight on her own without the aid of a special position, I covered her body once more in the basic missionary position.

But as my body molded to hers and my cock sank into the welcome of her outer folds, nothing felt basic about it.

Ready and waiting, she coated me, lubricating me for entry and bowing off of the floor in anticipation as she did.

"Look at me, Cal," I directed softly, positioning myself and waiting for her eyes to come to me before slowly pushing my way in.

Her tightness fought my intrusion, but as I watched her closely, I could see no signs of pain. Each inch solidified the moment and made my heart beat faster and faster.

I could feel hers beating the same pace, but in an alternating rhythm.

Together our hearts filled every moment of time, never allowing for an instant where one of them wasn't alive and active.

"Nik?" she called softly, her voice breathy but determined.

"Yeah?" I asked as I seated myself fully within her.

"I won't ever forget this."

My eyes closed tight, and my forehead touched hers. I moved my hands up her arms and linked our hands again.

When my eyes opened, I knew they were bright with affection.

"Me either, Cal."

"*Not ever,*" she insisted.

I shook my head and started to move my hips as I reiterated, "Not ever."

I knew it immediately. Her hot head and me, rational. The way she pushed when I pushed instead of shrinking back. The way she made me laugh and laughed *for* me like she wouldn't anyone else. I knew the things that made her tick, and she knew how to hook me.

This moment, this feeling, the way we moved in sync like we'd done it forever.

We were better—

★ CHAPTER THIRTEEN ★

Callie

Together.

That's how we always traveled to events in my parents gym, and the Olympic trials were no different. Most of the girls were traveling as spectators, or for a lucky few, as volunteers for the event. They'd act as runners for judges, communicating and shuffling scores, and getting water or other necessities. They'd help with the exchange of mats and equipment that needed to be moved, but mostly, they'd just get to live a childhood experience they'd never forget.

But coaches and gymnasts traveled in the same van, the same plane, the same train—whatever. It was one of the rules of the gym. And it hadn't changed even now, at twenty-six years old and two Olympics deep.

But this time, it meant something different.

It meant traveling with Nik.

As I stood in line behind him at security in Atlanta International Airport a little less than two weeks after the first time we'd made love, my hands itched to touch him. Just to hold his hand and brush the ridiculous hair out of his face.

The problem with affection had shifted, going from inexperience and insecurity with the newness of it to the inability to stop doing it in just the matter of that time. The scrutiny and limitations traveling with my parents imposed only enhanced that urge.

He'd been wearing his hat all day, but with security regulations he'd begun the routine of stripping down. First went the shoes and belt, followed by the hat and sunglasses he had perched atop his head.

His jeans still looked good, and the laughable plain white t-shirt party had yet to end. I guess it made his outfits easy to coordinate, and the switch from athletic wear to motorcycle garb seamless, but I couldn't help but laugh about it.

He heard me.

"What?" he asked, as he stepped away from the conveyor belt and into the line for the scanner machine behind several of the younger girls within our party.

They all laughed and giggled in front of him, too young to let the serious scrutiny of the TSA stop their antics for a second. My mom and dad had gone through first, so that they could be on the other end to keep track of everyone as they came though, and Nik and I were bringing up the rear to keep everyone together.

I could tell they were crushing on Nik, checking out his many assets and wondering what it'd be like to be with a guy his age. They weren't coached by him directly, as I took up all of his time, but it wasn't out of the ordinary for them to romantically idolize him even if he was.

After all, no one knew how attractive and talented he was better than I did.

Cognizant of his tendency to poke fun at my expense, I nearly bounced on my toes at the prospect of getting back at him.

"Oh nothing," I said loudly enough that everyone in the nearby area could hear. I waved a hand in front of my nose like a flag and scrunched my face in distaste.

"I was just imagining all the boys in the security office who just got a nice video shot of your fart."

"What?!"

The girls behind him covered their mouths and giggled, bringing their free hands up to their noses to guard against the imaginary smell. They probably actually smelled it too, such was the power of persuasion.

I continued on with ruse, smirking more with every ounce of annoyance that coated his handsome face. "They've got an infrared camera, you know," I explained with a smile. "It shows the cloud and everything."

"Cal!" he whispered, exasperated.

I bit my lip to stop my smile.

God, he was cute when he got annoyed. Maybe this was why he poked at me all the time.

When the girls moved through the scanner and out of eye and earshot, I scooted up behind him and fit my body to his.

"Sorry, dear," I apologized insincerely.

He smiled and shook his head, turning to look at me. "What the hell was that?"

I shrugged and put both of my hands on his hips. "The girls have a little crush on you."

He scoffed a laugh. "I'm pretty sure you can change that 'have' to past tense now."

My smiled through a facial shrug. "Probably. Good thing my crush is still very much present."

"Good thing, indeed," he agreed, looking around before pecking me softly on the lips just one time.

His feet moved into an easy jog when I shoved him gently at the prompting wave of the screener. He held my eyes until he couldn't anymore.

Hands above his head in the required position, the scanner scooted to one side and back again, and I used the brief window to admire the small strip of skin that had been exposed at the bottom of his t-shirt.

The process moved quickly, and I stepped into the machine just as a female TSA agent stepped forward to read my scan. Everything came back clear, and given permission to move on, I stepped forward to the conveyor belt and retrieved my belongings. Flip flops slipped on easily and my cross body bag passed easily over my head to settle on the opposite shoulder.

Nik was already halfway dressed, shoes on and his belt through the first three loops. My parents and the giggling set of girls stood ten feet away waiting.

I looked up to find my dad's eyes watching closely, so I didn't linger, instead scooting by a still dressing Nik and over to the waiting group.

One of the girls cleared her throat a couple of times after being pushed and prompted by the two others. I watched with curious disinterest until she finally got the courage to do what she intended.

It just so happened, the thing she intended was talking to me.

"Um, Calia?" she murmured timidly.

My eyes snapped into focus, taking in her sweet preteen face and the confident and mature way she held her body. In some ways, gymnastics forced you to grow up fast. It took more discipline than most adults could manage.

"Yeah ... " I paused, hoping someone would fill in her name.

"Amanda!" all three girls answered at once.

I smiled. "You're all named Amanda?"

Panicked eyes flashed between them as they hurried to explain. *"No!"*

"No, just me."

"She's Amanda."

"Right. Got it. So, just the one Amanda ... what's up?"

Her mouth curved up to frame her bright green eyes and a nervous hand reached up to twirl the end of her blond ponytail. "We were just wondering what it feels like to be in the Olympic trials."

"Yeah! Is it intense?" one of the others chimed in.

"Are the other gymnasts nice?" Amanda added.

I took a minute to think about it. "It's kind of the same as every other meet," I said. "Sure, there's pressure, but there's always pressure. And yeah, I've never met anybody there who isn't nice."

As I spoke, I felt Nik come up behind me. He kept his distance, and all accounted for, the group started to walk. My dad started up a conversation with him, but I found it virtually impossible to pay attention to them and the girls at the same time.

"But isn't it weird not to have your teammates there yelling for you and stuff?" the final one asked, speaking for the first time.

Almost at a loss, I tried to make the answer as upbeat as possible. "Well, I don't know. I haven't competed with a team there to root for me in a while. I guess it's probably a little different."

"We'll root for you!" Amanda promised immediately.

"Yeah!"

"Totally!"

The others agreed. "We'll make sure we yell real loud for you and everything," Amanda promised.

Overcome with emotion, my eyelashes fluttered with an unstoppable series of blinks and my throat tightened noticeably. Maybe because I hadn't expected it or I'd grown accustomed to going without it, but for some reason, the feeling of not only acceptance but friendship was so overwhelming it nearly brought me to my knees. I couldn't believe how wrong I'd been about everything and everyone and the way I related to them.

And it kind of made me wonder what else I'd so strongly thought was right, was really all wrong.

Somehow, I forced a smile. "Thanks, guys. That's … Well, that'd be really great."

"You got it, Calia!"

Finally to our gate, they settled into their seats and my dad ended his conversation with Nik on a handshake. My mom settled in next to the girls with a book, and my dad headed off to the bathroom or to get food or something.

Nik came and sat next to me.

"What did my dad say to you?"

He could tell I was worried and shook his head. His voice was low. "He just told me that he sees a difference in your gymnastics. Thinks I'm doing a good job."

"Wow." I frowned a little. "He didn't say anything to me."

He usually didn't though. He believed in punishment and critique but not so much in praise. I always kind of felt like it should be the other way around.

Nik tried to comfort me, doing so without touching me because of all of the prying eyes. "Hey." I looked back to him. "He noticed, right? And now I'm telling you what a good job you're doing. You don't need him to say it to you." He pushed his hands down the line of his thighs and sat back. "In fact, you don't need me to say it to you either. All you need is to say it to yourself."

"Thanks."

"Besides," he smirked. "I hear you got yourself an enthusiastic cheering section of eleven and twelve year old girls."

"You heard what they said?"

"Couldn't have tuned them out if I tried," he laughed. "High pitched."

I laughed. "Yeah, that's a twelve year old thing too."

He pretended to ring his ear with a shaking middle finger.

My dad moved to his seat beside my mom as our conversation came to a close, and with it came a change in our interaction. He kept his body angled away from me and the topic turned strictly to business.

He reminded me of all the skills I'd been doing really well with and what he thought to be the reasons, and I picked his brain on the things that seemed to give me trouble. My tumbling had been making steady improvements since I'd started tumbling with him at night. He had the best pointers and did a great job of explaining.

And when I was open to suggestion, he became endlessly patient. He didn't expect me to get it in one go, and he didn't get mad when I messed up.

He only did that when I stopped remembering who I was talking to and foolishly thought I knew better.

The sound of the gate check agent starting boarding forty-five minutes later was like music to my ears. I'd played it down with the girls, but the truth was, I was nervous. Big time.

People had expectations of me, and I had plenty of myself. This was my last shot at everything. My last Olympic trials, my last chance to do the best I possibly could.

I wasn't eighty, but my time was up. My body didn't have four more years to give, and more importantly, I didn't want it to.

Once on the plane with Nik seated next to me, I relaxed. My dad was on the other side of the cabin several rows back, and I finally felt like I had some time to decompress. I wanted to be able to lean on Nik physically and emotionally, and for now, I had to do it in secret.

Nik leaned forward and reached into his bag, pulling out a smaller brown paper bag from inside. When he sat back in his seat, he turned to me and smiled his most boyish smile.

"What?" I asked, knowing something was up by the way he was acting.

"I got you something. Just … for a little extra good luck."

My face pinked with excitement, and the bag landed in my lap with a thump as he dropped it there. "It's not much, so I don't want you to get overly excited."

"Shush," I demanded, unrolling the top of the bag and digging around until I came out with one of the items.

Bandaids. *All purple.*

Skepticism ripened my face and puffed the very tops of my cheeks as I dug around for the next item.

A keychain with miniature grips.

I smiled, thinking they were cute, but not knowing the reasoning behind them and good luck.

I shook the bag and still heard a rattle, and he nodded in confirmation that something was left, so I reached inside one last time and pulled it out.

A tiny bottle of New Skin Liquid Bandage.

My eyebrows pulled together in question.

He cleared his throat and shrugged. "Just stuff for your battered hands."

My eyes met his as he socked me with one of the most powerful gifts anyone had ever given me.

"So you can keep fighting and clawing and scratching. That stuff—and I—will be here to take care of you when you're through."

"*Nik*," I breathed out in a heartfelt whisper.

"Oh, wait," he called as if he'd just remembered. "There's something else too."

Confusion clouded my face. The bag had been empty after the New Skin. I knew it had.

Reaching over and grabbing that very item out of my hands, he twisted off the cap, and pulled out the handy little brush that was attached.

"Turn over your hand," he instructed, waiting for me to place my palm up in front of him. I did as he asked, smiling at the feel of his hand as it cradled the back of mine, and the precision with which he painted the thin layer of clear coating onto my skin.

But when I looked down, it wasn't clear—at least not entirely—a pretty purple glitter glinting out of the coating and off of my hands as the bandage dried.

"What ..." I started unable to finish.

He shrugged both of his broad shoulders and pressed his palm to the still tacky surface of mine. When he pulled it away, the a shiny, glittery layer of new skin covered both of our palms.

"Just a little extra magic."

And better yet, when I looked at it, I could imagine his hand on—

★ CHAPTER FOURTEEN ★

Nik

Mine.

She was mine, and I was hers. The way she'd looked at me thanks to a few stupid gag gifts had nearly blown my mind.

So much so, it had made the trip to Michael's first thing that morning to buy purple glitter more than worth it.

But I had to be on my very best behavior now. She'd been through five or six press interviews before this and was finally finishing up her last one. They all asked her the same stupid questions about being too old and too greedy, and at the repetition of them all, it wasn't hard to see why she'd formed such a skewed view of herself in the first place.

Finally, one of them asked a different question, but I wasn't certain it was better.

"Word is that you were outstanding in practice yesterday. That you've always been talented but taken it to a whole new level. If that's the case, what do you think has helped you reach such an unlikely peak at an age that's largely considered too old for the sport?"

Arms crossed on my chest and feet shoulder width apart behind the guy asking the questions, I rolled my eyes.

Callie's eyes came to me.

"My new coach. He's really helped me look at things in a different way lately."

My chest squeezed double the amount I considered comfortable, both affection and panic exerting their grip simultaneously.

Just as I suspected it would, the reporter's interest skyrocketed. "And who is your new coach?"

Callie gestured over his shoulder to me, and I did my best not to cringe. I didn't want her to feel like she'd done the wrong thing, but I wasn't excited about the new attention either. The more they watched me, the more I'd have to watch myself, marking my actions in some hollow version of their normal intensity.

I'd have to watch the way I looked at her and spoke to her, and I'd have to do even more than I already had to.

"Nikolai Bagrov," she touted proudly.

I smiled if only at the affection in her voice.

"He's the third ranked power tumbler in the world and makes my tumbling look like child's play."

I closed my eyes briefly in resignation.

The interviewer turned to me and back again. "What's he doing coaching you then?"

Callie went to answer, but I cut in and did it before her.

"I'm retired," I explained simply.

Callie's eyes opened wide in surprise, perhaps because I hadn't officially told her, or maybe because I spent all of my nights tumbling with her. She knew I was still in competitive shape, but from the moment my parents died, I'd been done. My heart still loved the sport but I didn't have the competitive edge.

I just wanted to have fun. And now, I wanted to coach Callie.

I'd deal with what came after that when I got to it.

I did my best to steel my face, schooling my expression in to one of dry disinterest. I didn't want him to get the inkling that there was something more or less to the decision or that anything about me was worthy of his interest.

The media on scrutiny was well and intrusive enough.

The interviewer shrugged, turning back to Callie to ask more questions.

With a nod and a jerk of my head, I signaled her that it was time to be done.

She understood.

"I don't want to cut you short, but I've really got to get going and get prepared for tomorrow," she explained with a sweet smile I recognized as fake from a mile away.

No one else was any the wiser.

I knew part of it was a genuine disinterest in the interview, but the other fraction of its plasticity came from me and her inability to get a read on why my mood had taken a nose dive into the shitter.

"Right, no problem. Good luck tomorrow," the guy agreed easily, knowing the long day she had ahead of her tomorrow and counting it as normal.

"Thanks," she replied, shaking the man's hand and coming to meet me where I stood.

"Let's go," I directed shortly, careful to walk beside her without touching her as I did.

She could feel the uncertainty wafting off of me, a nervous fidget making her normally smooth walk choppy. But this wasn't the place to explain, so I ignored it, walking with my eyes pointed on the ground as we weaved through the crowd in the lobby of the hotel, waited on the elevator, climbed on, and rode it in silence to the sixth floor and our rooms.

"My room," I directed, knowing that the possibility of her father coming to her room was much higher than him coming to mine.

"What?" she asked as soon as the door closed behind us. "What's wrong?"

"Nothing."

"Nik."

Frustrated, I ran my hands down my face, and then pulled off my hat and pushed them through my hair. She shoved my arms out of the way and stepped into my body, wrapping her arms around me and looking up with big eyes.

"What's wrong?" she demanded, concerned.

"Nothing, Cal," I non-answered.

She glared at me.

I widened my eyes in apology and opened my mouth like a fish before the words formed. "Really. I'm sorry for worrying you. They're just gonna be watching us now."

"What do you mean? They were always going to be watching us."

"No," I corrected. "They were going to be watching *you*. I was going to be just another part of the white, fuzzy background noise."

"Oh," she mumbled as she tucked her face into my chest , distraught.

"It's fine." The cotton of her shirt rasped slightly with the soothing motion of my hands up and down the back of it.

She pulled back enough to look at me again, forcing me to loosen my arms marginally. "I just didn't think it was fair that I was getting all of the attention when you're better than I am."

"I'm not better than you are," I denied.

"At tumbling?" Her scoff cut the otherwise silent air. "You *so* are."

I shook my head good-naturedly, my frustration easily replaced with affection.

Man, I was in deep with her.

"It's just hard not to touch you," I admitted, capturing the end of a strand of her long, brown hair and wrapping it tightly around my finger.

"Oh," she murmured, enlightened. "I understand."

Her arms tightened their hold, fingertips digging in through the material of my shirt and scraping at the skin underneath. I nodded at how in sync we were. Marveled at how our thoughts seemed to connect to one another.

"You're horny," she said simply.

Exactly.

Wait. *What?*

That wasn't what I thought she was going to say.

"No—"

"If you wanted me, you just should have said something."

"Cal—"

"After all," she said, widening her eyes meaningfully, "We're alone now."

Glancing around the dark room, I noticed the drawn curtains and the closed door and the utter silence from the rooms on either side.

Oh. OH.

I smiled and lifted narrowed one eye playfully, dropping my voice to a raspy whisper. "Do *you* want *me*, my little Pea?"

Nodding, she smiled in victory, and my body reacted almost immediately. "Like you wouldn't believe."

"Would you say that my fulfillment of this want is essential to your focus during the competition tomorrow?" I prompted with a raise of one brow.

"Yes," she agreed, bouncing her head enthusiastically. "Definitely."

"So, really, I'm just doing my job," I reasoned jokingly.

She pushed me to the bed, happiness radiating from her eyes

and straight into the heart of me, and broke me with one simple line.

"Come on, Nik." Climbing me like a jungle gym, she settled one leg on each side from the top. "Get to work."

"How are you feeling?" I asked as we lingered in the hall waiting for her name to be announced and the grand march into the gym to begin. Her mother and father were in the stands, and for that I was grateful.

I didn't plan to have any inappropriate conversations or picture the things we'd done the night before, but we had a routine.

Day in and day out we worked together alone, and that was what we'd become accustomed to. I needed her to feel free to tell me anything she needed to, and I needed to be able to do the same.

In one smooth move, she stood up from her bag and turned to me, lifting both of her hands in the position for a double high five.

I obliged without complaint or question, smiling just as she did when our hands came together and I felt the sticky indication that the gesture wasn't about high-fiving at all.

"Great," she said as I pulled my hands away and immediately looked at them. Purple glitter sparkled from the surface. "Ready to fight." I looked from my hands to her eyes, and that's when she finished. "Like I have a little bit of magic."

"I can't wait to watch," I told her truthfully, knowing it was going to be the likes of which I hadn't seen before.

She was more than ready.

The music of the march started, and knowing I had to, I stepped away. She forced her eyes forward and bounced her head to the beat, her tight, smoothed-back ponytail bopping as she did.

Her shoulders were low and her head was raised high, her feet pointed to precision as she began her elegant walk out to the floor.

The line surrounded her, some in front and the rest trailing behind, and when the majority of them cleared I stepped to the end of the hall and turned left to head straight for what I knew would be her first event. She was starting on Vault, what I liked to think of as her neutral event. I didn't expect her to bring in her highest score, but it wouldn't be bad either.

She'd recently learned to harness her power a little better. I waited to the side with the other coaches and glanced to the floor as they announced her. She looked up to the crowd with a smile and a wave, turning from one side to the other and back again before standing still back in line. Down the line like a wave, the rest of the girls followed suit in alphabetical order, most of them nearly ten years younger than she was.

Some glanced at her with curiosity, but the others stayed focused, keeping their eyes on the ground or blankly ahead of them, no doubt running through some form of detailed visualization.

It was a heady thing, coming to a competition where you had to show your best or risk losing everything. You could be one of the best performers in the sport at your home gym, but if you didn't leave it all on the floor on competition day, none of your fancy skills meant squat.

The introductions finally done, the floor cleared and gymnasts scattered in every direction. Callie came directly to the vault, going over to her bag that I'd carried over for her and pulling off her warm up suit.

Her leotard was still purple, the short clipped velvet of the suit portion fading into the mesh and sparkly sleeves with a gradual ombre effect.

She rocked her ankles back and forth, curling the toes of each foot into the ground and pulling back on her toes with her fingers, before bending at the hips and stretching her palms straight to the carpeted floor.

Bouncing to move the muscles further, she came back to standing, twisting back and forth at the hips and then finally throwing each arm individually across her chest to loosen those.

Drills took over, the act of throwing her arms above her head as if setting up for a skill nearly getting lost in a sea of girls doing exactly the same thing.

She wasn't the first up, so I walked to her instead of standing up by the vaulting table. I didn't intend to talk to her unless she talked to me because, honestly, she knew everything I could possibly say to her. She didn't need me to clog her head with a rote listing of the rules, and she didn't need me to know what was at stake.

She knew all on her own just by looking at the crowd and the judges and into the eyes of her competition.

All of these girls wanted it. Wanted it in a way that clouded the air and threatened to choke you with its oppression.

Think about the pressure you feel after studying for a test for a week, putting in the work and time and effort to do well, and magnify that times a million.

Every athlete there had spent their *life* preparing for this very day. Whether that meant twenty-something years or seventeen, it didn't get much more intense than that.

I pulled my eyes from Callie to watch Jillian Kristone take her turn on Vault. She chalked her hands and wiped her feet on the floor, cracking her neck from side to side, then practicing her set and twist.

I knew she'd be doing a Yurchenko two and half, just like Callie, what had become the new standard since every gymnast was capable of it in the Olympics four years ago. A skill that once seemed impossible now towed the line as the minimum. The progression was staggering.

The difference in scoring mostly came from the height and distance, as well as the form.

Jillian Kristone was one of the best vaulters in the country and arguably one of Callie's biggest competitors for the day. Large and explosive, she knew how to convert her body's energy into useful speed and blocking.

But where Jillian excelled in power, Callie dominated artistic merit.

And, thanks to a little pushing from me, my girl was looking pretty powerful in her own right.

With a salute to the judges, she scooted onto the runway, glancing at her mark on the thick foam carpet to make sure she was at the right distance. It was the kind of thing girls double checked and triple checked, Callie included, because one step off would be the bearer of more than one step of consequences.

Down the runway she went at a hard run, into her round off, backwards off of the springboard and onto the table, and up and off, twisting and soaring with great form and distance. She took a big step on the landing though, her power almost too much for the amount of rotation.

I looked back to find Callie looking on, a determined gleam in her eye and a smile hugging just the corner of her mouth.

She was in the competitive zone, ready, feeling the experience of having done this two times before and excited to use it to her advantage.

She climbed the stairs to the vaulting platform without a word, knowing she was next, and I did my part by walking down to the end of the platform with the table.

I climbed the stairs as well, adjusting the springboard to her positioning and making sure the mat was snug around it.

I cleared the space, going back down the stairs and standing back to watch as she repeated much of the same routine Jillian had performed. Chalk on the hands and feet, wiping the feet on the floor.

She did do one thing differently though, saluting the judges and looking down to check her spot, but stopping to look at her hands on the way back up.

My chest swelled and heaved as I glanced at my own hands. Excitement tore through my body at the same speed as her run, each step toward the springboard like a pound of my heart. Her body stretched in preparation, twisting into her round off, slamming off of the board and onto the table, blocking perfectly, and soaring through her two and half twists.

Her feet hit the mat and stuck as if suctioned to the ground.

Raucous cheers hit me like a wave, the crowd instantly on their feet to cheer for her.

I couldn't clap my hands hard enough or scream loud enough, the cupping of my hands around my mouth meant to help Callie, and Callie alone, hear my voice.

"That's it!" I yelled as she stepped off the mat and jogged down the steps closest to me.

She flew into my arms for a hug, and I embraced her fully, savoring the scant second before I released her again.

We walked together toward the other end where her bag lay on one of the chairs and her smile was infectious.

"Three more events like that, yeah?" I asked as she walked next to me, her hand on her hip and her breathing labored from the exertion.

She smiled and nodded, grabbing her bottle of water from her bag and taking a big swig.

Immediately, the lion's paws came off and the focus shifted. She'd be going to Bars next, and the preparation started then. It didn't matter what her score was or what had happened only moments before because it was in the past and nothing could be done to change it.

Not all gymnasts had the ability to compartmentalize like that, breaking a meet up into parts and separating them with bolted and locked doors once they were done. One fall on one event couldn't be the reason you crumbled, just as one success couldn't be the reason you lost focus.

Her grips came out of the bag along with a roll of pre-wrap and tape. I grabbed it from her hands without saying anything and directed her over to the side and out of the way. I helped her wrap both wrists, enjoying the opportunity to be close to her as I did.

Her score flashed on the LED screen that ran the circumference of the arena just as it blasted over the loud speaker. Her head came up to take a look at the fifteen point eight, but that look was it.

I could feel the camera over my shoulder, zoomed in on her face to get her reaction.

This was a huge event, and every moment of it would be immortalized on TV and internet everywhere. Maybe that was the reason we didn't say all that much. Neither one of us knew when someone was there or when the camera was on.

Callie didn't let it bother her though. She moved with the ease of someone watched and filmed twenty four hours a day for a reality show—like the cameras weren't there.

She had a steady hand and a focused gaze.

It was like she had none of the same monsters bullying their way around my stomach.

The thing I liked to call—

CHAPTER FIFTEEN

Callie

Nerves.

Raw and chewed out and used up, I finally reached the point where they got so active, I went numb.

Kind of like getting to the point where you have to pee so bad it goes away, or starving from a hunger so deep it stops.

That's what I was feeling for nearly the entire competition last night. I'd done okay.

Actually, I'd done well, but the whole thing felt like a dream. I floated around in my head so much I almost forgot where I was.

Success felt like enjoyment, but only when I saw the way it lit Nik's eyes and body up like a beacon. He was without a doubt my biggest cheerleader, practically running along the runway of the vault with me, jumping five feet in the air at the end of my routines with a ridiculous fist bump, and always waiting with uplifting and encouraging words for me when I rejoined him.

He didn't hover and tell me what I should have been doing or what I shouldn't because he knew I didn't need it. My mind was already crowded enough, all of the voices of my naysayers, supporters, my self-doubt and opposing drive, and the many hours of advice Nik had managed to cram all the way inside from the time he'd shaken my spit-soaked hand.

Now I was on the final event of the second day of Trials, and by some gift delivered straight from God's hands, I'd been given the chance to finish on Beam.

I knew most people wouldn't praise this kind of fate, but for me, it felt like home.

It felt like the best chance I had at finishing on a high note, going out with a bang, and earning a spot on my third Olympic team.

I expected Nik to give me some kind of check-in question to see how I was feeling or a pep talk to make sure I was ready.

But as he smiled at me with genuine warmth, affection, and pride, he only had one thing to say.

"I can't wait to watch you up there."

And, after hearing that, I knew I'd do everything I could to make sure I gave him one hell of a show.

Climbing the steps to the elevated performance platform, I looked to the apparatus rather than the crowd, the dull roar of its patrons sounding like the waves of the ocean. Louder it would roll in and softer out, over and over again as gymnasts around me set off their reaction with the biggest performances or mistakes of their lives.

Floor music started up in the background, a melodic beat chosen by someone else to accompany and showcase their gymnastics. But I did as I always did, using it as my own and transforming my body to match its tempo and rhythm. The mood would change mine, but only in the artistic sense of my routine.

Timing of a Beam routine is important, a predetermined length set and policed by the judges at each and every competition. That's what marveled me about my method, moving at different speeds on every occasion, even from last night to tonight, all based on the background music. And yet, I somehow managed to adjust and recalibrate each move to meld into the other, making my end come at a reliably uniform pace.

I greeted the judges with a salute and smile, stepping directly to the Beam in preparation for my mount and letting my hands hover. Once you touched the Beam your time started, and for me, a deep breath before that came to fruition was all important.

I closed my eyes briefly and shut out everything else, settling both open palms on to the top and simultaneously opening them again.

My feet left the ground courtesy of my arms, my press mount a perfect test of strength and body control in one.

The slightly roughened brown of the Beam stood out between my hands as it was dotted with white, the remnants of chalk from gymnasts past telling a story of its own. Legs and feet and hands all touched that surface at separate times on purpose and by mistake, a grip to avoid a fall and scrunch of an unsure foot's toe.

With one squeeze of my fingers I lowered back to sitting, swinging one leg through the other and using a one handed back walkover to stand.

Flourish and pizazz ended my movements by a flick of each hand, and my chin pressed high toward the ceiling. It's one of the hardest things for a new gymnast to learn, not looking down at a narrow piece of footing that all but screams at you to.

But that wasn't the way to succeed, the way to feel steady and at home. The key was moving on four inches just as you would on the forty foot floor.

I danced my way to the end up the line and pulled my feet together and my arms over my head. With one breath and swing, I set back into my back handspring layout layout series.

Each skill ended with my feet resolutely on the surface, no bobbles or balance checks to speak of. The routine flew by, each moment blurring into the next as if I was performing it in my own gym for Nik's eyes alone.

With only the dismount left, I tapped a foot to the end of the Beam behind me and gulped one breath. Roughly sixteen feet extended out in front of me, waiting to be eaten up by precision and skill and a blind-eye type of courage.

One foot in front of the other I moved into my round off back handspring combination and sprang off the end, looking to the sky in thanks when both feet landed on the ground and didn't move.

A sense of accomplishment rained down on me along with the noise of the crowd, but what stood out more than anything was the sound of Nik's ecstatic voice.

"Yes! Hell yes, Cal!"

I caught the sight of another fist pump as I rounded the Beam to the stairs, launching myself off of them and into his waiting arms. He hugged me big before letting me go and looking excitedly into my eyes.

"You did it," he said simply.

"We don't know the score yet," I reasoned, knowing that anything was possible and that feeling didn't always translate into score. And the feeling had been nearly legendary. Knowing Nik was watching me, knowing he was invested in my success and happiness and everything that came from the two together, I had totally *peacocked* the shit out of it.

But Nik was insistent, arguing, "You didn't see what I just saw, Cal. I *know* the goddamn score."

I looked to the score strip as I heard my name called over the loudspeaker, the flash of the fifteen point four nearly bringing me to the floor.

I knew my total score for the two days prior to this event, and I knew the standings of all the other gymnasts around me. A fifteen point four meant I had placed second overall.

Disbelief buoyed my heart and leadened my brain, the discrepancy between what I thought was possible and what was making me nearly come out of my skin.

Adrenaline surged when I accepted it, and I couldn't help but squeal as it all set in.

"Oh my God," I shrieked.

Nik nodded, a smile practically reshaping the features of his face.

I wanted to stay in that moment and take it in, but a flurry of activity separated us, pulling me toward the center of the arena and the ceremony that ultimately named me as an Olympic Team member.

I searched for Nik as it was happening, eager to see his face some more and share in the news, but the crowd swallowed him up and completely thwarted my efforts.

It amazed me how two things could go hand in hand so well together and at the same time be the cause of one of the most monstrous internal wars of my life.

The Coach and The Career.

Two things destined to go together.

But the way I wanted it wasn't as intended.

Two weeks back in the gym with Nik passed like the speed of light, and the eve of leaving for camp came before I knew it.

I tried my best to rush through every day in the gym just to get to the nights. Time when Nik and I would tumble together like always, touches and kisses in between, and flirting all the way through.

Every day I felt a burn, a fire that ate at everything I knew, setting it ablaze and threatening to make me rebuild.

I thought I would be scared of the flames, the memories sure to burn down, trapped in place that couldn't get out or be saved. I thought the heat of it as it encroached would make me cower in fear, that the change would feel unwelcome and cumbersome in an effort to start over.

Instead, the danger felt like opportunity, a chance to burn it all down and start over in a way that rarely existed.

Sure, material memories would be gone and my routine would change, but the world I created might have a chance to be bigger and better and all-together more well-built from the beginning.

Gymnastics was the old house, and Nik was the new. Both felt like home in some ways, but while gymnastics was built on opportunity and the dreams of my parents, my feelings for Nik felt mined straight from the deepest tunnels within me.

So when he asked me to go to the beach with him that night, I knew there was nothing I'd rather do.

Not pack for camp or spend time with my parents. Not dream about the coaches and gymnasts I would meet or the opportunities I would be given.

That night, all I wanted was him.

My hands sank deeper into the cotton covered flesh of his abdomen, and the muscles tightened noticeably in reaction.

His hand cracked the throttle to slow us as we pulled off on to the path and made our way to the back of the dune.

I pressed my cheek harder into his back and inhaled his scent mixed with ocean like a drug. The sea and the salt clung to my skin and his, and the humidity of the night made my clothes feel sticky.

Nik helped me from the bike before pulling my hand to his chest. "I can't believe you leave for camp tomorrow."

His words were congratulatory but sullen, the mix sounding funny to my ears. I understood perfectly though, the very feeling swimming and swirling in my own gut at ten times the power.

I didn't know how to make choices or decisions, and part of me felt like it should be easy to have both.

And if it had just been me and Nik in the world, it probably would have been. But it wasn't just us, the circus that was everyone else hanging out conveniently just on the periphery.

Nik helped me climb to the top of the dune, standing patiently in silence as my brain ran circles around itself for long minutes. When I made no move to touch, no move to speak, no move to engage whatsoever, he finally sought to find out why.

"What's going on, my little Pea?"

I shook my head at the nickname but smiled at the affection behind it.

"I just ... I don't know. I can't shake all of this inner turmoil, I guess."

"What's bothering you?" he asked softly, pulling me to sit down next to him.

Lightning bugs danced peacefully in front of us, and the sound of the ocean sang out a lullaby.

I sank into the comfort of it and him, leaning over to rest my head on my shoulder as I spoke.

"Everything," I answered truthfully. I hadn't only become this torn up recently. I'd always struggled with indecision and the demons in my mind. I'd just been covering it up a hell of a lot better.

"Can you describe it?"

He didn't scoff or tease or make me feel like a statement so broad was a joke.

He greased the path and eased the way, and he made talking about something I'd never even considered talking about before feel like the most natural thing in the world.

He made me feel open.

Scared the moment would pass, I forced myself to get it all out fast, practically piling one word on top of another until I got to the end.

"I don't take deep, heavy breaths just before sleep pulls me under. I think deep, heavy thoughts that cloud my dreams, awaken my mind, and muddy the blood in my veins. I feel insecure and unworthy and cyclically self-deprecating. Who am I to complain? Who am I to get trapped in the confines of my own head? I'm unbelievably blessed."

Picking up my hand, he laced our fingers and laid the back of it on his thigh. With a finger and thumb, he pulled my chin to him so I could see directly into his eyes.

"Blessed and blissful are two very different ideas. Things don't make you happy. Inner peace and bolstered self-worth do."

Understanding and acceptance swirled and swelled in the expression of his face, and the very same well-rounded nature that'd made me feel comfortable before made me snap.

I just couldn't wrap my mind around how he managed his thoughts and accepted my own as completely plausible no matter if they agreed with his or not. He didn't have to feel it himself to *get* it, and I envied the ability.

"How in the fuck are you so well-adjusted with two dead parents, and I'm fucked up while mine are very much alive?"

He cringed slightly, and my own reaction didn't take long to follow.

"Jesus." I dropped my head into the cover of my one free hand, lifting it and meeting his eyes again a few seconds later to apologize. "That was a terrible thing to say. I'm sorry."

"Don't be." He shrugged. "And it just is what it is. Internal battles aren't always dependent on the external. If that was the case, all kids from broken homes would lead broken lives, and every nurtured child would flourish." He shook his head. "That's not how it works."

"But a broken past makes it more understandable."

"Nah," he denied with a smile. "Just predictable and boring."

"I just feel like I'm sucked up in a tornado, spinning and spinning and hoping with all that I am that I'm gonna land somewhere soft."

He shrugged again, studying the rips of my hands and pulling them even tighter into his body.

"I know you feel mixed up and abused. I know you can't tell what direction is what, let alone which of them is right. But I think it's just because you need to slow down and take everything one step at a time."

He smiled. "Love is like over splits. You can't expect to give into it all in one sitting. But if you work at it, warm the muscles gradually, your body will eventually accept it as normal." The bulk of his shoulder nudged my much smaller one lightly. "It might even feel good."

Love?

The muscles in my throat seized and closed it off, shutting my mouth in a way that rarely happened anymore. I couldn't form a response. Racing and racing, the words and sentences fluttered through my mind without making sense and with a flat-out refusal to slow down so I could make an attempt to figure it out.

And as the moments passed, silence eerie and unavoidable, everything that was us came to a halt.

All of Nik's carefully placed and meaningful words—straight into the void.

It was cowardly and immature and indirect in a way that was so unlike the two of us. When we disagreed, we *did* it, telling one another, schooling one another, or in my case, emphasizing the point with a slap or a shove. But I couldn't bring myself to confront this talking point. I couldn't look at it, couldn't listen to it, or accidentally touch it with a ten foot pole.

I was leaving for training camp tomorrow.

It wasn't like I was off to war or anything, but it *was* a destination of isolation and distance. And it required a plentiful amount of focus that I couldn't afford to sacrifice to thoughts and wonderings about him.

He must have sensed my panic—it was hard to miss—and moved on without reproach or penalty.

The more time I spent with him, the more I started to wonder if he had been to some kind of saint training.

His patience seemed endless, the depths of its pool stretching all the way to the center of the earth.

Wanting to give him something in return, some confirmation that he meant something to me even if I couldn't find a way to say it, I leaned over slowly and settled my lips onto his.

A breath left his lungs almost immediately, a mixture of relief and happiness and satisfaction.

As much as we fought each other and as much as I fought myself, it all came down to this.

A connection, tried and true and real in every possible sense of the word.

Some people bring you peace and others mix it up, but what Nik showed me was that I had never really lived either.

Safe but unsatisfied, gymnastics had been just that as the years passed—a place to be.

I wasn't content but I wasn't scared either, and the combination of the two was enough to keep me there much longer than it probably should have.

His hands moved to my neck, pulling me up and into his lap, a leg straddling each side and my lips firmly on his. He kissed and I kissed back, opening my mouth to him and allowing his tongue to take control.

From turmoil to need, my belly shifted and coiled and begged me to give it some kind of absolution.

Down the front of my shirt, his hands skimmed the fabric with care and reverence, hooking at the bottom of the hem and retracing their steps up when they did.

The night was quiet and deserted, only the two of us and the sounds we made to keep us company. His groans fed my moans, and his touch mirrored the direction of mine.

My hands went to his hips, and his followed suit, squeezing and kneading my exposed flesh with the pads of his fingertips.

One hand left my hip to pull the shirt over his head, his skin clinging to mine with the damp of the air nearly immediately.

We moved together and apart, friction heating the connection and making my entire body flush with need.

He laid his shirt on the sandy ground and me on top of it, stripping my pants and panties in one smooth motion and kissing the path left exposed.

My eyes closed as his tongue lapped between my legs, and the arch of my back stretched as though on a tightening string to the moon.

The air around us shimmered, water droplets and lightning bugs and bright flashes of pleasure all mixing together to create one of the most impressive shows I'd ever been privy to.

He stood, shoving his own pants down and rolling on a condom, and then settled back between the waiting space between my legs.

His eyes held mine as he entered me slowly, his lips a scant millimeter off of the surface of mine. Our breaths mingled and mixed, concocting a new recipe of scent and sensation that I would forever associate with this moment.

A slow burn built in my belly, sliding into my limbs and spreading into my chest with each thrust. In a test of flexibility he ran his hand down my leg to my calf and lifted, up and out to the side and around, until the center of that muscle settled fully onto his shoulder.

My legs in a full split, I marveled at the feel of him, deeper and thicker and even more present in this position. I could feel his every inch, and he could feel mine, and the only thing that would have made it better was being able to admit that he was it for me.

That the rest didn't matter—not the things or the expectations or the people.

He started to shake, and his lips met mine, urging me to find my pleasure faster before he found his.

I pushed myself and fought it at the same time, wanting the ultimate high without wanting it to end.

"*Callie,*" he whispered, desperately close to his climax. The seconds immediately after seemed empty, desperate to be filled with more words of declaration. Of promises, of dreams, of love.

But I closed my eyes and let go, welcoming the freedom of my release as I orgasmed, screaming into the silence and breathing heavily into the shell of his ear.

He groaned just as I finished, my peak driving him to his with laser like precision.

I could feel him twitch and pulse inside me at the same time that my body held onto him and refused to let go.

Breaths mingled as we came down, kissing and pecking and sucking at each other with gentle affection.

His hands felt like heaven, and I'd finally gotten over the fear of using mine. They scratched and pulled at the smooth skin of his back, but he keened, relishing the feel and letting me know it.

Brief moments turned into long minutes as he reluctantly pulled out of me and lifted his weight to the side.

Looking into his eyes with the sky dark and glittering behind him, I felt complete.

Until I remembered something.

"I've just realized what we've done."

"You've *just now* realized?" he asked through a chuckle, smoothing the sticky hair out of my face and trying not to cover me in sand.

"No, not *that*. I knew we were doing *that* the whole time."

"Thank God," he laughed with a close of his brilliant blue eyes.

"I just remembered what you told me the first night we came here."

"What did I tell you?" he asked, at a loss.

"You know!"

"I'm afraid I don't, Cal."

"That you come here to be close to your parents!" I whisper-yelled.

His eyes widened slightly just as I spewed the rest of my panic. "You don't think they saw us, do you?"

"No," he comforted, wrapping his tan arms around me and squeezing.

My eyes closed in relief and my head settled onto the perfect pillow of his shoulder.

"They probably heard you though."

"Nik!"

"I'm just saying," he teased, and then mouthed, "Loud," directly against the salty skin of my cheek.

Feeling properly teased and content, I leaned into him and lie there, counting the stars and the bugs and the times the ocean rolled in and back out again.

I think I got to a thousand of each before I even considered moving, the late hour of the night and the pull of responsibility making me cringe all the way down to my toes.

"I just want to live in this moment," I admitted as we climbed on the back of his motorcycle to go back to the gym for my car.

I wanted to stay there on that beach with him and spend the night in his arms, and for now it wasn't a possibility.

I felt trapped by circumstance and freed by feeling.

I'd never felt this complicated in my life.

"Calia," my mom's soft voice called out of the darkness, sounding like a gunshot in the dead silent house.

My hand shot to my chest, and I took a panicked step back.

"Geez! Mom! You scared me."

Out of the dark and into the light, she padded softly from her spot in the living room to the opening in the hall. Her nightgown peeked out from underneath her robe, and the satin of her sash tangled loosely at her waist. Her feet were bare, and her long brown hair hung neatly in front of one shoulder.

She looked largely the same as she did every night, but her face held concern and worry that I wasn't accustomed to seeing.

My mom was a good woman. A good nurturer and caretaker and a good wife to my father. What she wasn't was outspoken.

She didn't get involved in my life the way my dad did, but she didn't stop him either. She just lived her life among us, watching us make decisions and hoping they'd turn out well.

Until now.

"Come on," she worried her lip, grabbing me gently at the elbow and pulling me into a walk. "Let's go in the kitchen and talk."

Her voice was low, and her eyes drifted up the stairs to where my father no doubt lay sleeping. This conversation was meant to be private.

Unable to deny her something she asked when she asked so little of me, I followed behind her obediently and took a seat at the table when she gestured that I should.

A pot of coffee sat waiting, and taking two mugs from the cabinet, she poured us each a cup before sitting down.

Her lips worried between her teeth for several moments, doing nothing but bolstering my own concern to near the point of breaking, before she finally found the courage to speak.

"I know what's going on with you, Calia."

My throat squeezed at her tone, but I forced myself to speak casually, without hurry, and as innocently as possible. "What's going on with me, Mom?"

"No," she shook her head, gripping her cup with both hands and still speaking in a whisper. "Don't give me that. Don't pretend you don't know what I'm saying. A mother knows. And you know exactly what I'm talking about."

I sank deeper into my chair, thinking about the feel of Nik's skin on mine and the sand that still clung to my body underneath my clothing.

Denial hung on the tip on my tongue, but with the feel of him fresh inside me, even desperate, I couldn't muster up a lie.

"I see the way he looks at you," she murmured thoughtfully. "And I see the way you look at him."

"Mom—"

"I get it, Callie," she interrupted, reaching out to take my hand in hers. "I get how easy it is to get caught up in someone when they're that caught up in you. I get that you're plenty old enough, and that you don't need your momma getting in your business."

When I started to exhale in relief, she squeezed my hand in warning.

She wasn't done.

"But I cannot ignore the consequences of this. I can't sit by and watch you throw away years and years and years of work. Do you realize what you're doing? What your father will think?"

"I can't just stop my feelings," I argued quietly, feeling my eyes well up. But the tears didn't fall. No matter how upset I got, they never did. I wanted to blow up. I wanted to cry and rage and argue about how none of it was fair.

How I didn't deserve to be punished for wanting to be with someone, for feeling like I'd finally found that thing people are looking for, the person who understood me and trusted me to understand him.

But I knew no matter how much I vomited my feelings all over the table and my mom, the talk wouldn't change. She wouldn't change her opinion completely and my predicament wouldn't disappear. It was here to stay for the near future, and no matter how angry I got, it wasn't something I could easily alter.

"I know," she agreed with a nod, forgetting her coffee all together and grabbing on to both of my hands tightly. "But can't it wait until you're done? You've got a month or so until you can retire. Just put it on hold until you're done, that's all."

God, Nik had asked me for virtually nothing, giving and giving to my needs and foolishness at every turn. All he wanted was me.

"I don't want to break his heart," I admitted to her.

I didn't want to break mine, I admitted to myself.

"He'll understand. If he cares about you, there's no way he'd want you to throw everything away that you've worked so hard to achieve."

Her words were a challenge. She hoped he wouldn't want me to, but part of her already thought he had asked. Or that he was trying to convince me. Nik was the villain in her scenario. No matter how she looked at it.

"He would never," I swore vehemently my voice breaking at the same time that my raw energy made the chair creak below me. He'd been the one to keep me alive, keep me from going so far down the damn rabbit hole that I couldn't thump my way back out.

"Then wait," she urged. "A month. It's so little time to sacrifice. It can't be worth it." She shook her head, convinced. "That amount of time with him cannot be worth the consequences."

I wasn't so sure.

A lot could happen in the span of a month. I knew that now.

Because the night had finally caught up with me, and my mind had finally made sense of all that jumble I'd been too scared to sort out before.

It'd been six weeks of back and forth, but one thing was for sure. I was stuck on Nik like some crazy strength glue, and I didn't know if it was possible to pry myself off.

I shrugged, pulled my lips to the side, and admitted one of the scariest possibilities I'd encountered in my entire twenty-six years. "I think I love him."

Panic flashed in her eyes, the danger that I was going to turn my entire world upside down burning in her brain. She couldn't let that happen. Because my world directly related to hers and my father's.

"Then think of him, Callie. Your father will fire him."

"You'd tell him?" I asked, my voice ringing with hurt and accusation and a tiny bit of uncertainty. I didn't know what would happen if it came down to that, and I didn't know if I could handle it when it did.

She considered it, looking deep into my eyes, and searching them for something.

When she finally found what she was looking for, her answer came out in a whisper. "No, Callie. You have my word that I won't tell him."

Air filled my shriveled lungs by extinguishing the blinding weight of my panic.

"Thank you."

"Just consider everything I've said," she urged. "Really think about it."

I nodded my acquiescence, and she reached out to pat my hand.

"Okay," she murmured, standing from the table and taking her untouched coffee to the sink and pouring it out.

Without another word, she left the room, tiptoeing up the stairs to avoid the squeaks and leaving me to consider how my world got so confusing.

Would it really be temporary if I said that word?

No matter how I spun it, I couldn't make the ring of finality change. It meant what it said.

It was what it was—

★ CHAPTER SIXTEEN ★

Nik

Goodbye.

I'd known we'd have to part ways as she got ready to head for training camp. I knew I wouldn't be able to talk to her and see her and touch her every day, but I'd expected the send off to go differently than this.

We were wrapped in each other, and her face was tucked firmly in my throat. It felt real and right—except for the way she shook, chattering in my arms as though she couldn't control it.

Her body strung tight to the point of breaking, she squeezed at my waist and tried to burrow closer and closer until finally, all of that tension broke.

Her body sagged and melted, but it wasn't in a good way. She didn't feel closer to me, connected to me, in the moment with me— she felt distant and gone and like she'd finally settled on the wrong side of a decision.

"We can't keep doing this."

I looked up at the unexpected words and pulled back out of her arms to see her eyes not on me, not open and honest, but on the ground. I kept mine on her and searching, willing her to lift them and look at me on her own. To come back into herself and the connection she *knew* we had with one another.

"Can't keep doing what?" I asked when her eyes refused to meet mine, a lead ball taking over all of the empty space in my stomach.

I knew where she was going, but some naive part of me hoped I could stop it. That she'd listen to me and herself and realize that each word she spoke came directly out of someone else's mouth.

"Us."

"Us," I repeated, rolling the word on my tongue and flicking a tone of disbelief off the tip.

"Come on, Nik," she whispered, her tongue flashing out to lick the dry of her lips. "I'm leaving for Olympic training camp. The back and forth, the arguing, all of *this* ..." She pointed between us. "*Sleeping with my coach*," she added, her voice hushed even more. "What about all of that seems healthy for focus? People are counting on me."

I *knew* people were counting on her.

I was one of them.

But my interest was completely different from everyone else's.

Unable to hold my tongue anymore, I asked the unthinkable. Something no person had ever dared to ask an athlete right before they headed to Olympic training camp.

Was any of it worth it?

"Why are you still here?" Her muddy, moist eyes jumped to mine in question. I didn't make her wait. "Still doing this? Because from watching you, from *feeling* you, I can't figure it out."

Her eyes jumped around furiously, trying to find her clarity, trying to find an answer she'd lost a long time ago, but potential tears never fell.

"I can't just be done. I don't know how I know, but it's not over. Something is supposed to happen. Something *significant.*"

Her words turned desperate, and her tone reeked of pleading. "It *has* to happen. You don't swim twenty-one fucking miles across the English Channel just to get in a boat fifty feet from the shore."

Accusation bled from her eyes, and distress and desperation morphed to anger. "I can't quit now."

"I'm not telling you to be done." My mind reeled, and hurt poured around my heart like fresh, wet cement. "Jesus, you think I'd expect that of you?"

"I don't know!" she yelled, confused and feeling trapped in her skin. I could see it in the agitated frenzy of her movements and the flush in her chest. She felt like she had no way out, no way to maintain both facets of her life and everything about it killed me.

It killed me to know she couldn't commit to something I felt so strongly about.

But mostly, it killed me to know I couldn't have her.

"What am I supposed to think when you say things like that?" she accused.

That I loved her.

God.

That was what she was supposed to goddamn think.

The words lodged in my painfully clogged throat, and I couldn't say it though. Not like this, not out of anger or spite or some last ditch effort to control a spiraling situation.

When I said those words to her, there would be no reproach or consequences. It would be me and her, and she'd damn well know before I said it.

"I want what you want, Cal. Not what your Dad wants or what's expected or what you think is the only option. I want you to be fucking happy, and I don't want it tomorrow or next week or four fucking years from today. I want it now, this moment, and I want it goddamn always."

"Goddammit!" she yelled, pulling at the skin of her face and turning away from me. "Why are you so good at putting everything together and making sense with your words when mine get jumbled and confused and come out all wrong all the time?"

I thought back to the many zingers she'd delivered in the past and couldn't say that I agreed. I never thought she'd had a problem yelling at me about what she felt, but maybe this was her way of telling me that's what was happening now.

I scrubbed a hand down my face and willed myself to calm down.

"Tell me what's going on, Cal. You just explain, and I'll listen." She turned back to me and her eyes searched mine. "I'll listen," I reiterated. "Okay?"

"I don't want it to be over," she whispered her heart splattered plainly across her entire face.

"Neither do I," I agreed, coaching myself to keep my spot, my distance, and not pull her into my arms.

"I just need time."

I expelled a heavy breath.

"Time to go to camp and concentrate on that and nothing else. I can't think about you or anyone else."

All I could bring myself to do was nod, wanting so badly to argue but knowing I'd do anything for her at the same time.

Even if it meant doing the one thing I had no desire to ever do.

"I can give you time," I forced out on a whisper, feeling my jaw hardened with frustration as I said it.

My words sliced open her chest, letting the relief, air, and bloody evidence of her turmoil spill out all over the place.

I worked to calm myself, knowing that she relied on me to be the calm one, the collected one—the one who could rationalize that not right now didn't mean not ever.

I started to form words several times, but none of them seemed like the right ones. When I finally spoke, it was to spew the only thing I could think to ask that didn't include begging and a profession of love.

"You know the exact mileage of the English Channel swim?"

She was surprised at first, but nearly instantly settled into the escape my simple question provided. She could concentrate on what was coming without me making it even harder for her, and the knowledge of it washed her pretty face with ease.

I knew I'd done the right thing.

She waved it off. "I wrote a paper once."

Awkward and uncomfortable we stared at one another as she rubbed the fingers of her hands together in anxiety.

"I'm sorry," she whispered, turning to leave without a touch or a hug or a kiss on the lips.

I'm not.

I couldn't change what was happening, but I wouldn't even if I could. Every moment with her was just a piece of the ultimate puzzle that we'd eventually get solved.

I didn't try to stop her, knowing this wasn't the end.

It wasn't for her, and it wasn't for me.

It was just a pause in time.

Just a little time—

★ CHAPTER SEVENTEEN ★

Callie

Off.

My gymnastics, my mood, my rhythm and tempo, and the way I tumbled—all of it had turned straight to shit.

Even Beam was feeling and looking wrong, several falls a day clouding my vision and throwing me for a complete loop.

And Coach Banning, the Olympic Team Coach, had noticed. But she wasn't the type to yell and demand, and for that I was thankful. Instead, she'd pulled me aside with a kind word—and a kick in the pants. Get doing or get gone. She wasn't mean, but facts were facts. Girls were lined up across the country just waiting to take my spot, and if I wasn't cutting the fucking cake, there was no reason to keep me.

Still, as nice as she was, I didn't end my talks with her feeling uplifted at all. I felt down and out and on the last leg of survival.

I always found that to be one of the most interesting things of the Olympic system, having to go from training with someone you know and trust to a stranger for one of the most important events of your life.

It was practical, that I knew, the impossibility of every individual team member bringing a different coach to the table nearly undeniable, but I still wasn't a fan.

The way I felt right now and the intensity with which I wanted *my own* coach reinforced it—I seriously wasn't a fan.

I missed Nik on all of the expected personal levels, but I truly missed him professionally too. He had become the strongest pillar of my support system and my go-to guy for advice. He had a head for the sport—both mentally and physically—and I trusted his instincts implicitly.

And, as a result, camp as a whole was a struggle.

I was grouchy and introverted and sullen at all the wrong times.

Which basically meant all the time.

The other girls noticed, since living and training and eating and sleeping together made it hard not to, and they tried their best to help. But without the ability to explain, without the comfort of his voice, I hadn't been able to find any kind of composure. And without those things, they hadn't been able to find a way through my brittle fucked-up shell.

There wasn't enough time for me to have a meltdown and do what I was supposed to do—which meant I needed to pick one.

We had a week to get to know one another, to mesh and jive in a way where our support was unconditional. We were used to competing against each other, but we'd be expected to be cohesive in the team competition and lift each other up.

But I didn't even want to be in the gym anymore, each day feeling like nothing more than a rigorous chore rather than the absolute privilege it was.

I thought again to the country-long line of muscular, vertically challenged individuals.

A ridiculous amount of girls would have traded all of their worldly possessions to be here, and I couldn't even find it in me to be thankful.

That kind of selfishness disgusted me even as I couldn't stop it.

"What's going on with you?" Jillian asked when I slammed my hand into the chalk bucket for the fourteenth time.

I hadn't exactly been a Chatty Cathy with any of the girls, but Jillian was the first to cross that dreaded line into crazy person territory. There was only one current resident.

And that was me.

My head dropped forward and pulled at my shoulders. Eyes clenched closed tightly, I took a minute to take a deep breath so that I wouldn't snap at her.

"Is it that obvious?" I asked her, looking up from the chalk into her twenty-one year old face and the blond hair that surrounded it. Her hair was in a messy bun on top of her head and pieces fell out from the gathering, splaying and curving down each side of her face.

A smirk pulled at her lips, skewing her features to one side and immediately cluing me in to what kind of person she was.

"Only if you're the chalk bowl. Or watching you. Or in the same building. Or, I guess," she shrugged, "alive."

A smart ass. She was a total smart ass.

For the first time all week, I smiled, the sound of someone poking fun at me like music to my ears.

I laughed. "I just … have some stuff going on in my personal life."

I wanted to talk to someone about it, but I knew I couldn't tell her. The very last thing I could do was *tell* anyone.

"You have a personal life?" she scoffed as her body went back on a step as though I'd shoved her.

A startled laugh nearly turned into a chortle before I got control of it. She'd somehow hit the nail on the head without actually know-ing any real information at all.

"Wow. I guess you're right. The problem is sort of in wanting one."

Her gray eyes narrowed, and I could practically see the wheels turn in her head as she calculated.

"Well, today's almost over. You should probably just give up," she suggested, ripping off the velcro of her grips and tucking them into one another. "I'll give up with you. We can go condition instead."

I turned to face her fully, smiling with my eyes and letting one corner of my lips pull up in solidarity.

"I don't think, in all the speeches I've ever received, anyone's *ever* suggested that giving up is the answer."

She waved it off with both hands. "They obviously haven't seen you in this state."

I shook my head and looked to the other end of the gym where Coach Banning worked individually with one of the other girls. The decision didn't seem possible, the fact that I was already walking a pretty thin line with the coach and committee weighing heavily on my mind, but in the end Jillian made it for me. She packed her grips away and gestured that I should do mine, and then began the walk over to the floor.

She pulled a mat over, crab walking it from side to side in or-der to be able to manage it herself, and slammed it down, the crack echoing and rippling through the gym until everyone looked on. She ignored them beautifully.

I needed her to teach me how to not care what people thought.

I was constantly considering what my parents and coaches and the media would think, often going beyond consideration and cav-ing as a means for cohesion. And when you let people grow accus-tomed to compliance, it's virtually impossible to escape that expecta-tion when you finally decide to have a mind of your own.

I was learning that the hard way.

Gesturing for me to go on one side, she went on the other.

"Come on," she demanded with a wave of her arm, sinking into an oversplit with ease.

I smiled again, a small bubble of laughter just peeking out from the opening of my lips. "You're demanding."

"I'm your friend."

Nik's words rang soundly in my head, the idea of giving in to Jillian and her friendship kind of the same as the way he told me to think about love.

Calmly, I sank down on the other side, settling into the splits both figuratively and literally, and this time I didn't feel the need to go slow.

Because I'd been warming the muscles for a while now, and the stretch didn't seem to burn nearly as much.

I could have a friend here. I could have Nik at home.

For the first time at camp, I felt like that might be true.

For the first time here, I didn't feel so—

★ CHAPTER EIGHTEEN ★

Nik

Alone.

I'd spent way more time than this in way more isolated situations.

And yet, with Callie away at camp, I was literally feeling like I'd never been on my own before. Eating meals felt like a chore and tumbling at night wasn't even an option. Normally, that was one of the things that helped me. Helped me piece together philosophical meanings and distinguish right from wrong.

Greased the wheels of my emotional discord and made my whole system work again.

In this case, I wasn't sure what was cause and what was effect. I felt mixed up and emotionally incomplete without Callie around to prove to me what felt right and what felt wrong. I would have used tumbling as a way to sort all of that out in the past.

But tumbling nights weren't *my* thing anymore. Not since she snuck around to watch me, and certainly not since we'd made love on that very floor.

Now they were *our* thing.

And so it seemed the solution had become a part of the problem. A stalemate of sorts where the only key was miles and miles away at Olympic training camp.

I'd considered sending her an email or a message, desperate for some kind of contact, but in the end thought better of it.

She'd asked me for space before she left.

The least I could do was respect it.

I'd been coaching some of the younger kids while she was away, and they were fun and dedicated to the sport. Talkative and loud and not at all flirty.

Which was a very *good* thing.

Adaptable to change and altogether amenable to all of my instruction, they made my job easy.

I was thrilled to know that Callie was coming back tomorrow.

Besides missing her challenge in the gym, I'd just missed her period.

Somewhat manic in my excitement, I searched for something to do. Something that made me think of her but left out the whole knife twisting in the chest. Motorcycle rides and trips to the beach considered and quickly rejected, I finally ended up here.

A swirling red and white pole twisted outside, and bad fluorescent lighting buzzed and hummed overhead.

A hipster-looking guy approached the chair behind me, unfolding a piece of fabric and looking me in the eyes through the aid of the mirror.

The plain black cape ruffled and rustled roughly in front of me as he shook it out, floating onto my lap and settling like a blanket over my body.

Around my neck it tightened, the feel of hands hooking it at the back of my neck and the way they had to weed through the hair making it even more obvious what I was there to do.

"Yeah," I confirmed when the barber asked what I was after again. "Short."

A decision made on a whim out of boredom and loneliness, I knew the results wouldn't go unnoticed.

And assuming that notice came from the right person, there was a definite appeal.

"Been growing it out?" he asked, finger combing through it with curiosity but keeping his opinion tucked well beneath the belt.

I looked at the long clumps of hair, the way they clung to the side and the front and did it in large numbers.

I remembered Callie admitting how stupid she thought it looked, and how she'd somehow managed to make me feel like that was a good thing.

"Not on purpose," I admitted and justified all at once. I'd never been conscious of its appearance before, but Callie made me that way.

It wasn't about vanity though. It was something more. It was about a combination of laziness and escape, hiding behind the hair and the curtain it provided for my protection from the outside world. I got less attention with it long and loose and *stupid looking*.

Cutting it off was like opening up an invitation to the wolves and admitting that I was ready to handle whatever happened as a consequence.

It was a good analogy for the way I'd handled my relationship with Callie, hiding and settling and accepting both milestones and rejections as they came.

But I wanted to be done with the rejections, even if that meant my belief and tenacity had to live inside my mind and heart temporarily.

I watched as he cut and combed, hacking at some sections with what seemed like a machete and selectively trimming at the very ends of others.

A transformation took shape, the grieving kid my parents left behind falling away to reveal the son my mom was proud to have.

All at once it felt like more than the hair, spiky and neat and unobtrusive in its positioning.

Out of my face and eyes, it cleared my vision in more ways than one. I could see what I needed and wanted, staring me in the face and demanding to be taken.

I didn't feel inhibited by obstacles. I felt free.

Free to take what I wanted whether her universe wanted me to or not.

When Callie came home, she wouldn't just be on her way back to the gym and her family and a coach who cared about her enough to let go.

She'd be coming home to a guy who loved her enough to hold on.

And I'd do my best not to—

★ CHAPTER NINETEEN ★

Callie

Let go.

Camp finally behind me, I had the opportunity to move on—go in a direction I wanted if only for a little while.

And the direction was clear.

I was homeward bound.

An already normally welcome concept, today's version had me damn near beside myself.

I couldn't wait to see Nik even if the way we'd left it was awkward. I couldn't wait to hug him even if as I was leaving I'd pretty much told him not to. And I couldn't wait to bask in him and his affection for as long as I could get it.

I'd worried briefly that he wouldn't forgive me or give me the opportunity to make up for my mistakes, but the truth was, that *wasn't* Nik. He wasn't the kind of guy who held grudges.

What he was, was the kind of guy who understood me inside

and out, even when the things he had to accept were my misgivings and transgressions.

And I was fully committed to making it up to him. I planned to do my best to show him how I felt without holding back and questioning motives and calculating consequences at every turn.

I didn't expect that I'd be perfect right out of the gate, but I had no doubts Nik would both recognize and appreciate an effort.

My mom had been pretty set in the notion that a month without him would be nothing. But after a little over a week, I knew with utter certainty that I disagreed.

I missed his smile and the lips that created it.

I missed his lively blue eyes and all the ways they told me what he was feeling or what he hoped to get from me.

I missed the way he poked at me and then harnessed the anger he'd created in order to use it for our passion.

And I missed the way he talked to me like everything I felt, no matter how ridiculous, wasn't, in fact, wrong, but instead couldn't be more right.

My eyes searched the gym, expecting to find him somewhere on the floor.

His motorcycle sat in the parking lot, shining in the sun and confirming his presence before I ever went inside.

But I didn't see him among the sea of other people. A rainbow of leotards faded and rolled into itself, mixing and matching and swinging across the spectrum as I scanned from one side of the warehouse to the other.

Disappointment sank my shoulders momentarily until the hair on the back of my neck stood on end.

"Hey, Cal," his smooth, rich voice whispered behind me, pulling my body toward his with the force of a flesh-sensitive magnet.

Ripples of sensation returned to my long-since numb chest and spread to my limbs, making my skin tingle and crackle with life and excitement.

A week-long trip to Olympic training camp, and the thing that sparked my mental and sensory pleasure was an everyday voice.

I turned to face it quickly, nearly tripping one foot over the other in the process.

My eyes bugged out, nearly all the way out of my head, the sight of his hair shorn to nearly an inch short surprising me enough to make me curse.

"Fuck."

"Shhh."

A laugh burst all the way from his chest as he urged me to quiet, the little ears and prying eyes of our meeting spot not even remotely appropriate company for a dirty mouth.

I'd gone over it in my head all week and all night and all the way home. I'd listed each thing at the sight of his bike and the swing of the front door as I'd entered.

I'd even gone over it again as I'd searched the gym for his face.

But as I stood there facing him, the list of things I'd missed was obviously one short.

"I never expected to miss your stupid hair," I said quietly.

He grinned, the change in his face turning him into one of the most handsome guys I'd ever seen. His voice was a whisper and his being nothing but a vessel of affection. "I knew I'd miss you."

His words touched me even as his hands didn't, but I'd had enough.

I knew I shouldn't and all the reasons I couldn't, but nothing could have stopped me from wrapping my arms around his shoulders in that moment.

Not *anything*.

He hugged me back without reproach, squeezing and breathing me in with ease and comfort and a face devoid of regret.

But he'd never cared about the consequences of our feelings. Not for himself anyway. His concern was almost always solely for me.

"Cal," he whispered into my hair, his arms cinching around me just a little bit tighter.

For once, I didn't have the willpower to let go, the dream of having him and everything that meant taking over my mind and outweighing any form of structured thinking.

Nik took the lead, pulling me away from him, but keeping his hands on the upper half of my arms.

My smile was goofy—I could feel it—and the cool skin of my arms heated through the fabric of my shirt at his touch.

"How was it?" he asked, genuinely happy for me and my accomplishments. I could tell in the size of his eyes and the way they pulled me in as if on the business end of a lasso.

I shrugged my answer because that's all I could do.

It hadn't been bad, and it hadn't been good. It'd been pretty damn neutral.

"I made a friend," I offered, hoping to touch on something positive rather than dampening the conversation.

"You?" he fake-scoffed, shaking a hand out in front of him and squinting one eye. "Friendly?"

"Stop," I told him with a playful shove. "I'm all kinds of friendly."

He raised just one skeptical eyebrow.

"Okay, so I actually made a friend by being the direct opposite of friendly."

His eyebrow descended to normal and then pulled in nice and tight, his confusion understandable.

"Jillian—"

"Kristone?"

I nodded. "Yeah. She's a real pain in the ass. Kind of like you. Poking and prodding and making fun of me every chance she gets."

He smiled and I mirrored it.

"So she was awesome?"

"Yeah," I agreed, my smile growing with each bounce of my nod. "She reminded me of you. Less philosophical speeches though."

"You love my speeches," he insisted and I did.

Not necessarily at the time he was giving them, but eventually.

"Nik—" I started as a fidget took residence in his body. His hands came together and apart and his feet bounced just slightly up onto his toes. His eyes were pleading and demanding, the way they always were when he really wanted me to listen.

"Tell me we don't have to stay here today, Cal," he breathed out finally, looking from me to the gym floor and back again. "I just want a few hours of you and me and nothing else in between. I don't want it to be about gymnastics or your parents or the things we want or don't want or can't have. I just want it to be me and you."

His hands tightened into fists as he forced out another breath. "But I understand if the answer is no, okay? I know you want time and distance until you finish this … maybe even after. I don't know. And I know how important this is for you—"

But it wasn't.

I'd made him feel that, even amidst the confusion and unknowns and fear and freak-outs, but the truth was, I realized in the scheme of things, a third Olympics wasn't all that important to me at all.

It was important to my dad and my mom and all of the gymnasts who looked up to me in the world. It was important to the media because my age made me a sensationalized story, and it was important to my National teammates.

But the only part important about it to me was finishing what I started and giving it the best I had to give.

By my standards, I was allowed a few hours to myself.

And in my mind now, anything that included me, included Nik too.

"Let's get the hell out of here," I broke in, sparing him the expense of telling me everything was okay that wasn't.

Happiness overtook his face, all of the lines and curves of its structure so much more exposed now that he'd gotten rid of the hair.

Short spikes shot up from the top, and the sides were clipped tight to the frame of his trim face.

Hammers beat out a rhythm in my chest as we turned toward the door and ran, his hand reaching out to take mine just before we reached the exit.

Somehow, the moment of caring about everyone else had passed and all that mattered was touching him, holding his hand, feeling the connection I so desperately craved.

I never looked back as we hit fresh air, the morning sun shining directly into my eyes the entire way to his motorcycle.

I curved my free hand around my eyes for protection but never slowed until we got there.

He handed me the spare helmet nearly immediately, shoving his own on his head and climbing astride the bike in what felt like record time.

I waited for his okay before climbing on behind him and settling into his back, the warm scent of his skin and laundry detergent rushing into my nose with each inhale.

He felt like heaven in my arms, and I made sure to let myself experience it. The body heat and life that pulsed through all of his visible veins and the way he crowded me back when I pushed into him.

I didn't hold back or hold out or try to keep myself contained. Instead, I let my heart bleed all over the white of his cotton, staining it with red marks of love and lust and admiration.

Because I did admire him. Who he was, how he acted, and his consideration for others.

Nik was a great person, no matter what category of relationship he was to me.

He'd been through enough in his life, but he put other people first without question and never belittled a feeling or circumstance.

If you felt it, Nik understood it—or did his very best to get to that place.

His back pushed back into my chest and cheek as we rode out of the parking lot, so I turned my head and touched the back of his shirt with my lips.

They pressed to his body firmer and firmer as I lingered there, the decreasing speed of our drive forcing my body forward and into his.

We were only a couple of blocks from the gym when he pulled over into a parking lot and shut off the engine. I was curious, but he didn't give me long to wonder, prompting me to climb off, pulling off my helmet and his own and slamming his lips into mine.

My breath left me in a whoosh as I sank into the feeling, a humming buzz turning my mind to drunken chaos.

His lips felt like the answers to every question I'd been asking, every emotion I'd been missing.

He filled my half-full heart up to bursting, taking his time, twisting and turning his head, and sinking deeper and deeper into my mouth and my mind.

No fervor seemed great enough as I tried to match his tongue stroke for stroke, the way his hands skirted down my body bringing the rest of me alive.

Thumbs pulled at the skin of my cheeks as he leaned into me, pulling my face toward him first, and then moving his hands to my hips to pull in my body when it didn't automatically follow.

Breath left my lungs in pants, the supply of oxygen dwindling more and more as time without air passed.

"Nik," I whispered as I pulled back and gulped in a fresh dose of life-sustaining nothingness.

His forehead landed on mine immediately, and his ragged breathing outdid mine.

"I missed you, Cal. More than seems right or necessary, but it's true. I don't know how it got this bad, but apparently I'm my very own version of Danny Zuko."

I shook my head against his, not understanding virtually any of the words he was spewing.

My head still spun from adrenaline and lust, and I probably wouldn't be able to make sense of anything for the next few minutes. But that didn't stop him from attempting to explain.

"The bad boy's long gone, and the hopelessly devoted version has taken his place."

"I don't think you were ever bad," I argued, missing the point completely by focusing on the first part of his statement rather than the last. He was just as lost in me as I was in him, completely willing to leave behind the person he was in order to become the person he was when we were together. It was a humbling notion and one I wanted to recreate within myself.

"I was never a hothead," he justified, "but I sure as hell wasn't good."

I laughed to myself, tucking my face into his chest before tilting it up with my chin against his collar to look at him. "I guess you are the coach who seduced his athlete," I noted, not really believing it for a second.

He cringed slightly. "Okay, maybe I had it backwards. I was a decent human being before I met you. Then I started preying on innocent—"

"Stop!" I laughed, shoving his chest enough to make his body rock back.

"Come on," he whispered, letting a smirk creep back onto his previously fake-distraught face. "Let's just go for a ride."

I nodded furiously, my agreement overwhelming my ability to give a normal response.

I wanted to just settle in and be close to him for a little while, feel the coziness of him seep straight into me, and I didn't feel like being in one spot.

I wanted to move and live and flit and wander.

And I wanted to do it with him.

"Calia," my dad called from the kitchen as I crept into the house that night.

It was starting to become a routine, the creeping and sneaking followed shortly by the scare of my life.

I had to think that one of these times my heart would actually go into palpitations.

As it was, I'd been lucky enough to keep it to a practice of skipping a beat or two.

"Hey, dad," I greeted back, turning the corner to see him sitting at the table going over some sort of paperwork. "What's up?"

His eyes met mine quickly before bouncing back down to the surface of the table in front of him. His reading glasses sat perched at the end of his nose, so I figured he was in the middle of something important.

"You don't need to come in early in the morning. I have some paperwork and meetings to take care of, so you can just come in in the afternoon for your workout, okay?"

"Are you sure you don't need help?" I asked, wanting to butter him up now for the day when I told him I wasn't everything he wanted me to be. If I ever got the courage.

"I'm sure."

"Okay," I smiled, thinking I could text Nik or go by his apartment in my free time so we could get together again in the morning. Free time was a commodity, especially these days, and I wanted to use it.

As I turned to leave, my dad burst my bubble.

"Actually, maybe you wouldn't mind helping your mother bake a few dozen cookies for a team gift? Since you have the morning off?"

His meaning was clear, and his words, despite the phrasing, weren't a question.

"Sure," I agreed, slightly disappointed but accepting all the same. I'd see Nik when I went in for practice in the afternoon and that would have to be enough.

Turning to go upstairs, he called me back once more.

"Whoops, almost forgot, Cal. Sign this real quick."

"What is it?" I asked, no stranger to my dad handling paperwork for meets and endorsement offers and the like.

"Just something for the Olympic committee."

"Oh, okay."

I grabbed the pen off the table and daydreamed about Nik.

And at least we'd had—

✭ CHAPTER TWENTY ✭

Today.

I felt rejuvenated in my purpose, and I planned to use all of the hours provided to help Callie find her form.

She'd told me she'd had trouble concentrating at camp without me there, and as much as I enjoyed the flattery, I hated that that was the case.

I wanted success for her every day whether I was there or not and the training for that would start today.

I tucked my helmet into the saddle bag, snapped it closed, and walked with a bounce in my step to the front door and through it.

My mind a tunnel of focus, I paid little attention to anything and everyone else and headed straight for the bathroom to change.

"Nik," Frank called from his open office door, stopping me in my tracks with surprise.

"Yes, sir?" I asked, turning to face him but not changing the direction of my lower body.

I didn't want to give him the idea that I wanted to stay and chat, but I could hardly disregard him either.

His eyes narrowed.

"Come in here, please."

"Okay," I agreed, pointing to the gym. "I'll just go tell—"

"She's not here," he interrupted, waving me toward the office with large, snappy swing of his hand.

My eyes shrunk and pulled together at once, knowing by the tone of his voice and Callie's absence that something was up. I just didn't know what yet.

Dread boiled like hot lava in my stomach, coating the inside and slowly sliding its way out in an attempt to take over everything. My breath caught before I could answer, half wondering if I was ready for what waited beyond his door.

We'd had meetings before, but this one felt notably different. It felt ominous and obscure, and I wasn't sure if that feeling was completely contrived or a vivid depiction of my intuition.

Whatever it was, it wouldn't wait.

It wouldn't disappear or change, and the best thing I could do for my nerves and sanity was get it over with.

"Okay," I finally agreed, turning and heading for his office right then.

He stood in the door as I entered, shutting it resolutely behind me and rounding the desk.

"Sit," he ordered.

Slowly, I sat.

Moments passed with nothing but the muted sounds of a full gym whispering through the glass and the whirring of his desk fan behind him filling the air.

I wasn't sure if he was trying to force my hand with the stress of the wait, but it wasn't a good plan for me. I didn't plan to say one fucking word unless prompted.

"You know, Nik, I brought you here because the prospect of having someone of your caliber coaching in our gym was beyond appealing," he finally started, clasping his hands over the tent of elbows on his desk.

I didn't like where this was going. Sure, his words were mostly positive, but the tone … well, it was *not*.

It leached acid and spewed disdain and spit out a healthy dose of accusation just in case the first two weren't enough.

"I thought you'd be able to relate to Callie, help her learn to listen and apply what her coaches enforced."

"Yes, sir." And I thought I'd done a pretty damn good job. She'd been better than ever at the Olympic Trials and every day besides, her practices in the gym as well as her performance on the world stage a testament to how well my coaching style jived with her talent.

"If she could listen to you, I figured she'd listen to me and her National Coaches."

I didn't move, didn't speak because, to me, there was nothing to say.

He was talking about her like a dog or a child, a basic skill set like listening and obeying something to be learned instead of accepted, and Callie sure as hell wasn't either of those.

I could see his jaw hardening in time with my own, his inference and my non-response pushing each other's most sensitive buttons.

When the tension broke, he finally put it all out there. "I didn't give you permission to date her."

Leaning forward slowly, I settled my elbows onto the arms of the chair and linked my steady hands together.

"All due respect, sir," I enunciated clearly, slowing down each word to make sure there was no confusion or misunderstanding when it came to my answer.

"But I didn't ask for it."

The rubber band on his cool snapped, bringing his body up and over the flat top of his desk until all of his imposing weight leaned viciously into his hands.

"Doesn't consent mean anything to you?" he asked, angry, his veins standing out in his neck and a purple hue under-lighting the thin layer of skin.

"It means everything to me," I told him honestly, staying in my seat to appear as far away from confrontational as possible given the circumstances. I didn't want to be disrespectful, but I did want to prove my point. And I wouldn't settle for agreeing to something I didn't think was right.

"And Callie gave me one hundred percent of hers."

That's not what he meant though. For him, Callie's permission and his were one and the same—but only when the order came from him.

His thoughts were written in the mottled purple splotches across his face and chest, and the inky abstract of their illustration read like a murder mystery novel where I was the victim and he was the killer.

"That's—" he started to yell.

"And I'm sorry, sir," I interrupted, "but when it comes to a relationship between me and your daughter, her happiness is the only kind that matters."

I don't know what I expected, but I know it was infinitely more positive.

To me, my reasoning was sound. Completely bulletproof in its simplicity and beneficial to Frank as the first man who had loved her.

But what I thought and what was weren't one in the same, the mood and atmosphere in an already struggling room doing nothing but tanking.

"Well, it's done," he declared as though he had final say. Like what he said, went—period.

But I wasn't his daughter, and I hadn't spent my life trying to please him. I wouldn't go so easily.

"It's not," I disagreed calmly, telling him the truth and admitting to my intentions all in one painful shot.

"I'm telling you it's done," he reiterated, and I finally lost a little bit of my cool.

"I got that, sir. And I'm sorry, but I don't give a fuck. It's not done. And it probably never will be."

He sighed deep and heavy, before grabbing a piece of paper off of his desk and shoving it toward me.

I read over it quickly, and the gist had me about ready to lose my shit.

"A letter to the Olympic committee about misconduct?"

He said nothing.

"What in the fuck good would this do you? It's the exact thing you claim to be trying to avoid!"

"You're right. That's where you come in."

I heaved an angry breath and moved my fist open and closed, trying to calm some of the rage. My normal even keel was slipping away piece by piece thanks to what I now had no doubts would be the worst fucking father-in-law on the planet.

"If you go, there won't be a letter, there won't be anything. Nothing but success and the unheard of achievement of three Olympic games for Callie. But if you stay, with the way she's running around with her head lost in you, this is going to happen one way or the other. At least this way," he said, shaking the paper in front of my face, "is on *my* terms."

I'd never wanted to punch a man so badly in my life, my normal instinct to reason completely overwhelmed by a need for a fight.

But it wouldn't do anyone any good for me to fight it now.

Most of all, it wouldn't do any good for Callie.

"Blackmail?" I asked, unwilling to believe he'd treat the fate of his daughter so callously and impersonally. I wanted to believe I was missing something, that there was some other clause he'd kept just to protect her.

His simple shrug said there wasn't. "Whatever it takes."

My hands shook as I looked out the window into the large space of the gym, unbridled, never before matched fury rattling the ends of my bones together and heating my normally cool blood to a boil.

Unaware of the conversation on our side, gymnasts and coaches smiled and laughed and carried on with their days. All the while, my world spun out of control.

I felt sick to my stomach, truly moments away from throwing up every last spoonful of the oatmeal I'd had for breakfast, the whole dirty thing screaming of poor decisions and unintended consequences.

I knew there was no clean break to this scenario, no get out of ramification free card, and no going back to the way things were.

I could only move forward, and the ugly choices presented to me didn't make accepting that easy.

But, as the hamster in my mind spun and spun on its wheel, my heart had to step up and make the decision for it. And only one thing felt right.

After everything I'd witnessed today and up until this point, only one person deserved to make this decision and it wasn't me and it sure as *fuck* wasn't the dirtbag in front of me.

It was Callie. The one who had the most to lose and gain and a hand in most of the variables.

My instinct was to protect her, sure, but by doing so, I'd be doing her the same disservice as her father.

I swallowed thickly, clenching my jaw and keeping my eyes averted from his face.

I couldn't even stand to look at him.

"It's up to her," I murmured, knowing that talking to her about this would be my only chance to come up with some other solution.

"She's already agreed," he said simply, the words echoing in the room like three individual gunshots.

Each one, a direct. Fucking. Hit.

Another sheet of paper shoved out in front of me. Blood started to seep from the holes, shock the only thing keeping me alive for the time being.

"That's why she isn't here," he explained. "She's agreed to my terms, agreed not to see you until the Olympics and any and all endorsement deals that follow are through."

My teeth ground into my jaw and the sounds of the gym turned toxic. Tears threatened, and if Frank hadn't been there watching me, I probably would have let them flow.

"She's worked her whole life for this, Nik. She cares about you, that much is obvious, but she didn't want to have to face you with this choice," he reasoned with saccharine sincerity. "Make it easy on her."

I took the page from his hands with a rip, studying the lines of her name at the bottom and willing it not to be so. But those were her curves of script, her lines and loops and cute dots above each 'i'. She'd written her name in the chalk on the mats and in the sand at our beach enough times for me to know.

I wasn't mad at her.

God, I wanted to be.

It would have been easier and infinitely less messy for my heart.

But instead, I was just broken.

After everything that had happened between us, all of the push and pull that we'd fought and shoved through until this point, I'd thought we were past this. Yesterday, that work and fight felt justified. She'd given me real emotion and connection, and she hadn't held back. The metaphorical parking lot had been entered, and the "Don't Back Up Or Die" spikes were fully engaged.

I'd read the Warning Sign, but I couldn't stop myself from being pushed back across them without consent.

My emotions were shredded nonetheless.

I understood the things that were at stake and the pressure she felt to live up to each and every one of them.

I *got* it.

I just wanted and hoped and believed the solution was going to come from a different direction than this.

My heart ached at the lack of a goodbye, but I knew with the way I was feeling, it probably was for the best.

He shoved a nearly identical agreement meant for me in front of the other one, and I was helpless to do anything to stop it.

"I'll sign," I barely whispered, the effort to squeeze any words through my throat, let alone those, greater than any physical challenge I'd ever faced.

I grabbed a pen from his desk, took the piece of paper, and did it without looking back as a furious and unrelenting sting attacked my nose. My tongue felt too big for my mouth, and I choked on the thickness of my saliva, but I ignored it.

The longer I lingered the harder it'd be, and if there was one thing I was interested in doing, it was making things easier for Callie.

"Good," Frank muttered as I finished, grabbing the paper from my hands and putting it behind him on his desk. "Now get the hell out of my gym."

"Gladly, sir."

I pictured my dad's hand on my shoulder, guiding me through one of the toughest moments I'd ever faced as a man.

A moment where I wanted more than anything to let all my anger out through punches and slurs and the behavior of a boy.

A moment where, for Callie, I needed to be a—

★ CHAPTER TWENTY-ONE ★

Callie

Good man.

It took twenty-six years and basically no looking—but I'd found one.

He'd practically fallen straight into my lap, and what a good thing that was since I had absolutely no time or prospects for meeting him or anyone else otherwise.

I was feeling good as I walked into the gym that afternoon, three batches of cookies baked contributing to a healthy amount of raw dough consumed.

It supposedly wasn't good for you, and my father certainly didn't approve, but I'd enjoyed every second of it.

Glancing back at Nik's empty spot in the parking lot, I wondered what was keeping him.

As the glass door swung closed behind me, I hitched my bag higher on my shoulder and headed straight toward the locker room to put my things away.

A few of the homeschooled gymnasts were scattered about the apparatuses, pointing and flexing and running at full speed depending on where they were.

Just when I got to the edge of the half wall that separated the front-of-house from the floor, my dad's head popped out of his office door.

"Cal?"

His face was an unreadable mask.

"Yeah, Dad?" I asked, wondering how he'd known I was here so quickly.

"Come in here, would you?" he told me while pretending to ask.

Eager to get it over with and knowing Nik wasn't there, I changed directions and headed directly into his office. I couldn't imagine what he wanted and the last thing I felt like doing was having a sit down with my dad. My good mood would surely be ruined by all of the things I should be doing.

He shut the door behind me, gestured that I should sit down, and leaned up against the wood edge of his desk.

The fake leather of the chair I sank into was warm to the touch, and the air in the room felt oppressively hot.

My heartbeat sped up to compensate for the extra energy used to cool myself down, and I had to choke my way through several shallow breaths.

His eyes were watchful and assessing, and I got the distinct impression that his mood for this particular talk was anything but warm and fuzzy.

"What's going on?" I asked when he didn't say anything.

"Why don't you tell me, Calia," he said, using the full version of my name how parents tended to do when you were in trouble.

Searching my mind, I tried to put together some sort of a progress report, but it was hard when I didn't know what I was looking for. "I don't—"

"Sleeping with your coach!" he interrupted with a boom.

I shot back in my chair as though I'd been slapped.

While I sat stagnant, tongue-tied with surprise and the absolute worst kind of dread, he was the one to find his voice again first.

"Do you have any idea what kind of scandal this would be?" His voice was quiet in volume but sinister in intensity and meaning.

I tried to form words, to defend myself *and* Nik, but nothing I had to say happened fast enough.

"You'd be ruined," he declared in my silent void. "The media would turn it into a fucking circus. You'd be slut-shamed and he'd be labeled an opportunist weasel. You might even be kicked off the Olympic team for misconduct, I don't know."

They couldn't do that. Could they?

I didn't know the exact rules, but I couldn't imagine that a consensual relationship between two of-age adults was grounds for legal action. But the truth was, I really *didn't* know. I knew what I thought everyone would think all along, that it was inappropriate and a precedent for crossing a very technically tricky line, but I had no clue when it came to the *actual* ramifications of our relationship from a rulebook standpoint.

My mind reeled and roiled, and my stomach's behavior wasn't far behind.

I felt sick, like I could ralph right there, right on the floor at his feet, and when I thought it couldn't get worse it did.

Fear, foreboding and powerful, washed over me at the realization that Nik's absence was so out of the ordinary, so unlike him, *so* something he *wouldn't* do.

Not today, not any day, and not unless he hadn't had some kind of choice.

"What'd you do to make him go?" I whispered, knowing it had to be true.

Knowing he *wouldn't* have left unless he'd been forced to. Counting on it and waiting for confirmation because I *needed* it.

"Nothing." My dad's voice was like a whip, meant to lash and sting with every strike. "I explained the options, and he *chose* to go."

"No," I whispered, not believing that everything we'd been through, everything I knew about him, and all the things he'd helped me learn about myself could culminate in something as hypocritical as this.

He would have spoken to me. I *knew* he would have.

I shook my head, swallowed roughly, and blinked at a rapid pace. "He would have—"

A paper landed in my lap, unwelcome, just as my dad's words overpowered my own.

"He signed an agreement, Cal. No contact with you whatsoever until the games and any subsequent contracts are through."

I shook my head as I looked at his name, staring at me mockingly from the bottom.

My dad softened his voice and squatted down in front of me.

"Look at it this way. He obviously cares about your future a little, agreeing to start over so you won't have to."

Disbelief and hysteria swirled just under the surface until I couldn't stand to sit still any longer.

When I jumped up, it forced my dad out of the way, his back hitting the edge of his desk, but that didn't slow me down as I grabbed for my phone from my bag and pulled it out frantically.

I jogged out of the office without another word, my father calling my name behind me as I went and my hands shaking violently all the way.

I didn't stop, unwilling to compromise and unwilling to believe Nik wouldn't be waiting on the other end of my call.

Pushing send as I shoved out the main door into the parking lot, I brought the phone to my ear and listened to it ring with time with a series of full body shudders.

Four rings and a click left nothing but disappointment to greet me on the other end.

From the top of my head to the bottom of my soles, every inch of my body felt alone and cold in a way it never had.

Because now I knew what it was like to have it.

And you never truly missed something until it was—

★ CHAPTER TWENTY-TWO ★

Nik

Gone.

As fast as my two wheels would take me, I flew down the road headed for nowhere.

Nowhere to go and nowhere to be, the loss of my parents weighed its heaviest since the day it happened.

I drove toward their old house without thinking, without considering that it wouldn't do me any good, and with no regard for the laws of the road.

It was the only place that made sense in my heartbroken chest and rationale rattled mind, and I couldn't think of a better idea than the three hours it took on my bike to get there.

Wind whipped and welcome rain stabbed me with its force.

Storms raged around me and within, the inability to make sense of going from feeling like I had everything to nothing in an instant, churning in my gut and mind like a Category Five hurricane.

My mind a mess of loss, I sat and watched the new family in my old house for a couple of hours like a creeper, pretending the lights going on and off from one room to another were the doing of my parents. I could picture Callie there, meeting them, laughing with them, and largely benefiting from their unconditional love.

But I didn't have them, and I didn't have her, and the vision of their meeting would never happen anywhere outside of my fantasies.

Numb from the overexposure, I didn't even feel the rain as it beat into my already soaked clothes and my eyes stayed open in the world's slowest blink.

I could see my father dancing around my mom with the technical skills of a professional dancer and the smile that would light up her face as a result.

But mostly I saw the freedom with which they lived their lives, so openly affectionate and obviously in love and unwilling to let anyone tell them they couldn't have it.

They'd known what it was like to give up everything and start anew only to find they'd really had nothing to begin with.

What they had with each other—*that* was everything.

Frustrated with my delusions and ghost stalking, I finally gave it up, heading for the only place I knew I could.

With a few knocks on the deep burgundy door, feet padded and plunked their way down the hall to answer it and the barrier swung open to my friend Connor.

He hadn't seen me in three months.

The disappearing act I'd pulled after selling my parent's house had been a necessity at the time, and because of everything I'd had with Callie, I'd never regret it.

But I wasn't proud of the way I'd skipped out on Connor.

"Nik—"

"Hey, Con," I said, knowing I looked like hell and I sounded worse, and knowing that the simplicity with which I greeted him was far shy of what he deserved.

"Nik, man, it's good to see you," he told me with heart, his voice both of steel and affection at once. He turned the other direction so his voice would carry further.

"Carli!" he yelled to his wife. "Nik's here!"

I heard a pot drop in the kitchen just before the sight of her rounded the corner.

Her violet blue eyes lit up and she barreled down the hall, slamming into me with the full weight of her body and making her long black hair swing out and around my shoulders like a curtain. She ignored the wet of my body and hugged tight, squeezing me like she meant it.

"I think she's excited," Con joked, smiling at me like I hadn't been one of the shittiest friends on the planet. It felt good in a way I hadn't even known I needed, lost in the lows of heartbreak, to know even when I *felt* like I had nothing, I still had people willing to give me their all.

"Listen, Con," I said, setting Carli gingerly aside with a smile. "I'm sorry—"

"Don't even finish that sentence, man!"

"Yeah," Carli agreed, stepping away from me and into Connor's side like I hadn't just soaked the entire front of her body. "We saw you on TV at the Olympic Trials! I just about flipped my shit!"

She looked to Con and asked for confirmation. "Did I not just about flip my shit?"

"She flipped her shit," he repeated by command rather than by opinion, smiling and fighting his hand on her shoulder as he did. She slapped him on his.

Memories blazed as if surged by an influx of gasoline.

Just that one move made me happy and sad at the same time, and I'm not too ashamed to say I almost cried right then.

"What are you doing here?" Carli asked with disquiet, finally connecting the dots between seeing me on TV and the fact that standing there with them was exactly where I *shouldn't* be.

"It's a long story," I admitted, scrubbing a hand down my face and feeling bad for barging in on them.

Connor was the first to jump in to help me change my mind. "Well, come in! We've got chicken quesadillas and cake and a whole hell of a lot of time."

Part of me didn't want to stay, but the smarter part knew it'd do me good.

So in I went with a muttered 'thanks' and a smile, following them down the hall and into the kitchen like I did it every day.

I wished Callie were with me right then, her hand in mine as she trailed behind me.

Her laugh. Her smile. Her goddamn eyes.

All of it poked at me and pushed, and within a few minutes, I couldn't think of anything I'd rather do than tell Con and Carli everything.

There was so much to tell, so much to feel, and so much to miss.

But every step of it was worth it, every memory a reward for the burn, and I healed a little bit with each word I spoke.

Because I didn't just remember the way I felt.

I remembered the way she did too.

There was a validation in that and a hope. A possibility that if I wanted it badly enough and fought for it, I still had a chance.

I wasn't telling our story as me, and I wasn't telling it as though there were an end.

I was telling it—

★ CHAPTER TWENTY-THREE ★

Callie

As us.

Each skill, each event—I lived all of it as an us.

It'd taken me the full week since he'd left to get here emotionally, but I'd finally done it. I'd gone through all of the stages of a meltdown; heartbreak and rage and giving everyone I encountered at any point in the day the finger.

It took the realization that I could still connect with Nik because I held a piece of him on the inside, trapped tight in the center of that big beating organ in my chest, to realize that I did absolutely no one any favors by not getting my shit together.

Not me.

Not him.

And most certainly not *us*.

Hands painted with New Skin glitter, I carried Nik everywhere with me and listened to him yell for me in my head as if he were there.

I told myself what I wanted to hear, that it wasn't the end, but instead a hiatus, the reality that he wouldn't have been able to come to Brazil with me anyway only helping a little.

Bodies bounded and flipped, skills being practiced and run-through all around me. Lights flashed off of cameras in the stands, and fans waved hand-made signs back and forth.

I was amazed at the presence of our support, a strong-hold of USA fans taking over nearly an entire section of the arena and deafening the rest of the crowd with their cheers.

Jillian warmed up next to me.

She was one of the only other girls competing on every event, the one person to place ahead of me at the Trials, and the pressure on us to lead and anchor the largely younger team was immense.

"Are you alright?" she asked, knowing I'd been a different person since team practices had started up when we arrived.

"Yeah," I assured her. "No worries." And I was okay. I wasn't great, and I didn't think this was the way I wanted it to be, but I was focused. I was ready to be what I needed to be for her and the team and for myself—all the years I'd put in needing to ultimately be worth something.

I laughed and gave her a playful shove, teasing, "Come on! We're starting on Beam! It doesn't get much better than that!"

"Oh. Yeah," she grumbled. "My favorite."

Genuine laughter drifted from my mouth to my ears, the absolute shock of it waking me up and putting me in a good mood for my routine. I hadn't laughed like that since the falling out, and until then, I hadn't even known it was possible.

I gave her a wink and a nudge as I climbed up onto the platform and she yelled slightly offbeat but encouraging advice from behind me.

"You got this! Don't get your hands confused for your feet!"

"Float like a butterfly, stick it like a G!" And after little to no re-action. *"You know? Like a knife? And a gangster?"*

I laughed to myself as I rubbed chalk between my hands and onto the soles of my feet, bouncing on my toes and cracking my neck in anticipation of my salute.

My tongue flicked out to wet the dry cracks in my lips, and equally parched air seemed to catch in my throat. I tried to be cool, calm, and collected, but in some ways, I knew it wouldn't be possible.

Not many people could say with certainty that *this* could very well be the last time they'd complete a routine for the world to see. But I could.

I'd decided that I was done at the end of the Olympics, no matter the outcome, no matter the pressure, and no matter the opinions of others.

And by done, I meant done. No endorsement deals, no show-case meets, no training on the side.

Tonight, I'd give all I had to give. And at the end of the Olympics, I'd officially retire.

There wasn't any reason to hold back on the last exercise of the workout. It was the perfect time to give all of my energy—all I had—to being the very best I could be.

My arms flashed up over my head with a flourish and down again when prompted, and a smile stretched across my lips in perfect sync.

It wasn't so much that the smile was real when a gymnast salut-ed, it was more of the whole idea of putting on a show.

Peacocking, as Nik would say.

I smiled for real then, the thought of him teasing me with a smile warming and settling my nerves.

Hovering hands turned into a base for my mount, my weight settling over top of them and balancing on a perfect counter point system. The angles of my body changed as necessary for support, and a slow ascent ended with a pose at the top.

My motions moved along quickly, following the tempo of the floor music as I always did and making sure to use a fluid system of effortless transitions between skills I liked to think of as checkpoints.

Each routine had a set of requirements or skills you were expected to perform, the variances and difficulty subject to the gymnast who was performing. The stuffing, or what you put in, as well as how well you actually executed each move were combined to give you an overall score.

The averages varied by event, but Beam was a lower scoring apparatus by a long shot.

I prepared and relaxed, sinking into my legs and bounding back into my series, each skill separate but interconnected in importance. You had to finish one before you could begin the other, a misplaced foot without an escape a danger that could really end up getting you hurt.

But part of the score came from connectivity, and that didn't just happen by magic. It happened with repetition and faith and a whole lot of muscle memory.

Half of the time my brain didn't have time to think what I was doing all the way through, my memory and reflexes no doubt delayed even further by my age.

But the muscles—they were where the ease originated, their movements almost practiced into undirected submission.

I could hear Jillian's cheers as my feet hit the mat, the other girl's voices blending together in similarity. To me, they all sounded the same.

I knew that sounded like a terrible thing to say, but that wasn't how I meant it.

What I did mean, was that they were distinctly a unit, whereas Jillian and I tried to carry ourselves above and beyond and as figures of authority.

Given my mental state, it was damn near laughable, but I could guarantee when it came to being here in this moment and doing what I needed to do to not let anyone down, I was giving it more than my all.

Jillian high-fived me on my return, the other girls converging on the two of us and bringing it into a huge group hug.

I reveled in it rather than resented, knowing I wouldn't be in this place again, with this kind of single-minded group initiative, not ever.

Still, I wondered if Nik was watching, if he wished he could talk to me as much as I wished I could talk to him.

With the intensity of my own feeling, my own insatiable thoughts and desires, I didn't know if it was even possible.

"Floor," Jillian said simply getting in my face at the first sign that my mind was starting to wander. I needed to leave Beam *and everything else* behind.

"Yes, ma'am," I said with a smile and mock-salute.

I got the distinct impression that she was mentally giving me the finger.

Maybe even a double.

Sort of a one stone, two birds kind of thing.

One look into the crowd reminded me though, one, two, or four, the birds and the stones were welcome. Because words hurt a lot worse and lasted a lot longer.

My dad looked on with a smile, my mom tucked neatly under his arm, but for me, one look at him took me back.

All I could see was his office. All I could feel was the pain. All I could hear were the words that haunted me over and over again.

He agreed. He agreed to—

★ CHAPTER TWENTY-FOUR ★

Nik

Start over.

As I watched her on the floor, all I could do was hope for more and wish that I could call out for her to start from the beginning. Not because she'd messed up or done something wrong, but because she'd done all the things right.

Her arms floated like an extension of her eyes and her feet moved with sure, swift steps and jumps from one place to the next. Her musicality was spot on like always, the sound of the song transporting her to another place that she replayed directly on her face.

The zoom of the camera made me feel like I was there, and Con and Carli were starting to make fun of the results of that fact.

"Dude. Do you think you can back away from the TV just a few inches so the two of us can actually see what she's doing too?"

I only half listened to them as she moved though, focusing on the smirk on her lips and the heave of her chest just before each tumbling pass.

She flipped and flew with control and precision, harnessing the power like I taught her and turning it into just the right amount of energy. Height and distance didn't mean loss of control, and by watching her tonight, I knew that she'd mastered it.

And despite the distance and the circumstances, her victories still felt very much like my own.

Not as her coach, or her mentor, or someone who'd taught her anything about gymnastics.

No.

As I watched her come alive in front of millions and millions of people, I felt it in my chest, in my connection.

Right in the heart of my pride and love.

Ironically, the heart of those two things felt exactly like the heart of me. Center-left in my chest, under the skin, muscle, and bone, and rooted permanently through a complex interconnected system to the rest of me.

"Nik," Carli said from right next to me, her small hand settling gently onto my shoulder and applying pressure.

"It feels like me out there, you know?" I said, talking to her and myself at the same time as I realized the reason everything felt so mind-bogglingly powerful.

She shook her head slowly, a small frown of apology marring her normally proportional features.

I smiled and shook my head. "It's just ... an investment in her," I struggled to explain. Her successes were mine. Not because I'd helped her achieve them, but because her success and happiness was what I genuinely wanted most out of life.

She nodded then, thinking she understood. "You put in a lot of time and effort coaching her. I'm sure her successes feel like your own."

"No," I disagreed strongly, shaking my head for emphasis. "It's not that at all."

I looked to the ceiling and back again, an ache in my chest making my hand float to the space above my heart without prompting.

"It's … Callie was broken when I met her." I smiled, forcing my jaw to unclench. "Beautiful, God, so beautiful, but without pleasureful purpose and drive and lost inside her own head. But the toxic thoughts that haunted her weren't her own. They were the seeds planted there by everyone else who put her out in the fucking boat destined for the big show and left her to drift."

I shook my head, my chest both tightening and lightening—a combination I'd foolishly long thought impossible—as I talked.

"A woman like her? She doesn't know how to drift, to fucking wander, to dream and reason and find her way when nothing feels fun anymore." I corrected myself. "Or she didn't. But now she does, and not because I taught her how or did the leg work or any other fucked up thing. She's that way because I told her it was fucking okay. *That's* it."

Carli hollowed her cheeks and sucked at her lips to keep a tear from escaping, and I clenched my jaw against the onslaught of tears of my own.

"Years of unhappiness and pressure gone." I shrugged my shoulders and lifted one corner of my mouth. "All because I gave her permission to let it fucking go."

Connor murmured low and slow in the silence that followed. "Dude."

"It sounds messed up and twisted and, I don't know, maybe it's because I don't know how to just be her coach, or just be with her, and instead they're unchangeably locked together, but I'm so fucking proud of her I can hardly stand to be here watching her and not be able to tell her."

Carli wiped away tears and turned directly to Connor with accusation. "Why don't you talk about me that way?!"

His exasperated, pissed off eyes were just what I needed to break the tension, letting me turn back to the TV and watch with wonder as Callie got ready for Vault.

Chalk clung to her entire body at this point and a tiny line of concentration had formed directly between her chocolate eyes.

They looked directly into the camera then, holding it as if she were looking directly at me before lifting her hand to look at it.

I willed the camera to zoom in on the skin, to show me a mix of purple and pain, but it cut away and focused on someone else before there was even a chance.

A bar routine complete by someone else, the camera cut back to her, the back of Jillian's blonde head taking up most of the frame. Callie laughed at something she said and I found myself smiling along with her.

I'd gotten ahold of myself at this point, so I scooted back from the TV, settling onto the couch and watching like a normal person.

She shoved Jillian like she normally shoved me, climbed the stairs to the platform, and started her routine of chalking the majority of her body.

The palms of her hands and the bottoms of her feet, as well as the insides of her legs. No friction was good friction, smooth and fluid motion the only way to go when competing on Vault.

Her ponytail swung playfully as she leaned her head back and forth to stretch her neck, doing several set and twist drills in a row.

Her face was a mask of concentration, and like always, her pink tongue came out to wet her lips.

With a salute she stepped onto the runway, double checked her spot and worked her feet until they were flat into the heels. With a push and a bounce to her toes she was off, running and lunging into her round off with precision, back handspringing onto the table and blocking perfectly through her shoulders.

With force and precision she forced her chest up to assist in rotation and looked over her shoulder and pulled tight for the two and a half twists.

The camera cut to the back of the Vault for her landing, three lines positioned on the mat to assist the judges and gymnasts alike. It made it easy for both of them to gauge the landing, to find their positioning on a landing that was blind.

Her toes curled into the mat and fought, forcing what seemed like the unstoppable force of her body to an immediate end.

The roar of the crowd was almost as loud as this living room, Carli, Connor, and I all yelling and screaming as if she could hear us.

A neighbor banged on the adjoining wall of their condo, but Carli just ran over and banged back, a roll of her eyes and a toss of her hair reminding me what being with Callie felt like.

"One more event to go," I told the room at large, the USA in position to take first. I thought about the prospect of a gold medal for Callie, and I almost couldn't stand how good it made me feel.

"How's she on Bars?" Connor asked, interested and doing a good job of distracting me from missing being in person for Callie's celebration.

You wouldn't have been there anyway, I chided myself.

Individual coaches were treated like spectators at the team competition of the Olympics, sectioned off behind a wall with all of the others. And I had a feeling her dad would have taken that spot.

"She's good on everything," I told him, shaking myself out of my inner thoughts and watching her tighten the velcro on her grips.

Jillian went first as the leadoff, and Callie was meant to be the anchor. Much like swimming, coaches often stacked the lineup to set the tone they wanted. A leadoff was often the most consistent, not necessarily bringing in the highest or the lowest score, but reliably bringing one in altogether. And the anchor was meant to seal the results, to hold the team in place with a routine that built on the scores of the other gymnasts and ended on a high note.

All it meant for me, under these circumstances, was that I had to watch everyone else before I got to watch her.

Jillian impressed like always bringing in a solid routine and setting a positive tone for the event. Everything was on the line, and you needed a big hitter for big stakes. Jillian was it.

Being that this was the team final, there was only one girl in between selected to compete along with them for their total score, and I'm ashamed to admit I didn't even remember her name.

On a normal basis, yeah.

While I was waiting to watch Callie compete her final routine in one of the biggest meets of her entire life—no.

I shook out the nerves as her routine came to a close and Callie climbed up onto the platform to take her place.

I watched with amusement as she chalked her hands, spitting into each palm on the international stage in front of millions upon millions of people.

I watched her rub chalk into the palm of each grip, clap her hands together, and then start over again, and I watched all of it with rapt attention as if she was doing something worth watching.

One final breath, she moved to the front of the Bars, waiting to be prompted for that all important salute.

Her hands flashed above her head and a genuine smile painted the line of her lips.

I held my breath as she started her first skill, kipping and casting and hooking her feet to the low bar for a nearly full rotation that catapulted her to the top.

Her casts were precise and the placement of her hands was dead on. Not even a sheet of paper could fit between her trim legs, the muscle perfectly and calculatedly pressed together in a showing of excellent form and concentration.

She was killing it, making my heart beat a mile a minute and painting a smile so ridiculous across my face, I was glad no one but

Connor and Carli could see me. Each time she hit her handstand at the top of her rotation it was like she was made to do it—like a string pulled taut at just the right moment and yanked her perfectly pointed toes straight to the ceiling.

She was doing it—what she'd set out to do—showing the world and herself that twenty-six wasn't too old. It wasn't past the prime.

She had never been better.

Knowing what was coming, I eased myself up off the couch and paced toward the TV, preparing myself nearly as much as she had to be. As her hands left the bar for her Piked Tkatchev, I held my breath knowing she'd be going straight into her Deltchev immediately after.

But it didn't come.

She left the bar beautifully but traveled too far to form a comfortable grip on her return, and I could do nothing but watch as her fingers stretched to hang on, prolonging her swing and changing the angle of her body.

I reached for her as though I could actually catch her through the TV, but her fingers left the bar unplanned and unhindered. She tucked into herself like someone practiced at falling, but the momentum was too much to combat, and the very apex of her neck and spine struck the ground with a brutality that nearly made me sick.

Her body crumpled into itself before slowly unraveling into a state of stillness I'd never seen it take on before. Her lifeless legs lulled open and her empty, grip-covered hand fell to her side and unfurled.

Every normally vibrant indicator of consciousness was absent, and the immediate silence of the crowd and announcers settled hauntingly into my bones.

My first instinct was to go to her immediately. Just drop everything, run straight out the fucking door, and not even bother turning back.

Thankfully though, I gave myself just a moment to think it

through and realized that would be about the dumbest thing I could do.

Carli grabbed me on one side and Connor took the other, chaining me like a wild fucking animal, but I'd already figured it out on my own.

Reasoned it in my head and heart and fucking accepted it just like I did every-fucking-thing else.

"Cal," I whispered to myself, watching her on the screen and sinking to my knees in order to pray for a miracle. All I could do was ask for everyone that was there to help her. I couldn't ask them myself, so I asked God to deliver a message for me. I didn't pray often, and I didn't use language He would be proud of, but I believed. In that moment, I believed and I did it as hard as I could because I had to.

I was helpless to do anything more.

She was in Brazil, for fuck's sake.

I scrubbed angry hands down the tears on my face.

It wasn't like I could be there for her now, in this instant. It was going to take me at least a day to get there. Guaranteed. Between getting on a flight, getting to the airport, actual travel time, and finding my way to her once I got there, I had a long road ahead of me.

One I fully intended to traverse, but I'd rather do it with some information.

Stepping closer to the TV, I watched as a crowd of people worked on her, willing her to give me some sort of sign, some sort of indicator that she was okay.

"Come on, little Pea. Give me something. Move. *Please move.*"

Mindless of distance and futility, my fingers sought the skin of her wrist, touching the highly pixilated virtual depiction of it lightly. I willed her to feel me despite impossibility, to give me just one fucking thing I asked for.

She didn't.

Disregarding the past had done me no favors. History—despite hope and mental sorcery—

✭ CHAPTER TWENTY-FIVE ✭

Callie

Repeated.

Over and over I pictured his face in my head.

His eyes were like actual pools of water—moving, flowing, and changing color along with depth. Each time his focus shifted, so did mine, zeroing in on a new fleck of deep blue and trying to help it float through the much more abundant aqua. Their magnetism made it hard to focus on his words, but I wouldn't have traded those moments spent studying their nuances for all of the words in the dictionary.

Sure, looks were shallow and words could mean everything, but in those split seconds when his eyes changed before my own, I would have sworn on my every Olympic medal it was the opposite.

And right now, I needed the comfort of that feeling. I needed it to swaddle me in its warmth and make everything feel right again.

The word wrong had never been a concept worthy of my focus,

but as I tried to make sense of what was happening, denying its existence was no longer an option.

Up felt like down and left very nearly tricked me into believing it was right.

Voices called out to me constantly and on repeat, but none of them were the one I wanted. Like they were speaking through water, every pronunciation of my name seemed foreign and unwelcome, and my brain did nothing but scream another.

I tried valiantly to talk my uncooperative body into bending to my will, but for the first time in my life it *wouldn't*.

Digging deep down into my sternum, I found the last vestiges of my energy and willed them into one single action.

Into one single word.

"Nik."

Priorities shifted and silence mocked me.

My entire life had been a series of events all specifically driven toward this very moment. I'd known all of my work was meant to culminate in a flourish of glory and significance. I'd known there'd be a second in time when I knew why each part of my life had played out the way it had.

I'd *even* known it would probably happen now—on this stage, in front of all of these people.

I'd just had the timing wrong by about three minutes.

But I knew now.

This was it.

This moment of reflection and clarity forced on me by the inability to move made it fucking impossible to deny.

He was everything.

"Calia," I finally heard, the sound of Coach Banning's concerned voice finding its way through the muck of my confusion.

I didn't answer though.

I tried.

214

But the chain of communication from my brain to my lips was obviously hindered by a temporarily broken link.

God, I hoped it was temporary.

"Callie, listen to me. Do *not* move," she instructed, making me mentally roll my eyes.

I wasn't even responding vocally. Moving seemed pretty fucking unlikely. But, given the grave look on her stricken face, I decided to take note of the memo and put an asterisk next to it. Move it up to the very top of my Don't Do List.

With my options for activities dwindling, I tried again to make sound vibrate properly off of my vocal chords.

"N-N-Nik."

No one paid me any mind, but I wasn't sure if it was because they couldn't hear me or that they just had more important things to worry about. Everything seemed surreal to the point of feeling out of body, and it made it nearly impossible to discern whether or not the things I thought I knew were worthy of validation.

Whatever the case, after several ventures with nothing gained, I decided it wasn't worth the effort anymore. I knew he wasn't there to answer, and none of these people knew we had a relationship other than coach and athlete. I'd thought it was important to keep it that way, and as was my nature, when I willed something, I settled for nothing else.

That was why I was here in the first place, competing in my third Olympics and largely ignoring the ailing cries of my overworked body. I didn't know when to say Uncle, and now, with the feeling in my legs eerily absent, my body was screaming it for me like a plane on fire with both wings broken off.

I could, however, feel my arms, and, having just rolled me up in order to carefully place a backboard beneath me, they were strapping them tightly to each side of my body with thick velcro straps. I figured if there was ever a time to cry, this would have been it.

Instead, I focused on a single, floating particle of chalk, the brilliance of its perfect white shining starkly against the obscurity of a faceless, silent crowd. It fluttered and flipped aimlessly, waiting for something to catch it or get in its way.

I hadn't lived even one second of my life that way; conversely, I worked hard at sprinting from one place to another. I mentally berated myself for aspiring to be like a fleck of chalk, but the absurdity of its unimportance was largely overshadowed by the truth of it all.

I liked to think it was my dad's fault. That'd he'd pushed me to this.

But I really had no one to blame but myself. Because my dad was just pandering to the version of myself I'd allowed to run rough-shod over what could have been a fucking life.

I'd been the one too cowardly to admit to him and myself that plans had changed.

By focusing all of my energy on each destination, I'd done a pretty good job of ignoring the journey. I'd competed in three Olympic games for shit's sake. And all I could think about was making a bigger splash than each time before.

Ha, I thought as the paramedics took positions at each end of the board, my immobile body sandwiched in between. *I'd sure as hell done that.*

I watched as my piece of chalk met another, flitting and floating together then from one place to the next and landing safely on some asinine surface connected to one another.

I was surprisingly unaffected by the fact that my gymnastics career was over, and had ended in a fall no less.

I *was* worried about the lack of feeling in my legs, but when I really considered the consequences that stretched out in front of me, there was only one thing I was scared to death not to have.

And that was—

★ CHAPTER TWENTY-SIX ★

Nik

Nik.

A gentle shake to my shoulder woke me from what could only be described as a fitful sleep.

"Nik?" the flight attendant asked, having learned my name after looking at me with what I guessed was a reflection of my own sad eyes and asking.

I'd driven like a madman to Atlanta to catch the first flight in time, not grabbing clothes or belongings or more than the passport I thankfully kept on my motorcycle all the fucking time. It would have cost me a round trip of about six hours which wasn't the end of the world, but it very well could have meant the difference in my precarious mental health.

Despite my parent's loose affiliation with their international relatives, they'd always carried theirs with them just in case and preached the habit to me.

International travel took time, something I was finding out for myself first hand, and they always wanted to be ready and able to get there as quickly as possible if something happened.

In my entire lifetime, I'd only known of it happening one time, for the death of my Grandfather.

I didn't go with them, as I'd never met the guy, and the reception when they got there wasn't exactly warm, but my parents believed in doing what was right—even if that meant doing the opposite of what was easy.

"We're about to begin our initial descent."

"Thanks," I murmured, sitting up taller and wiping an agitated hand across the sleep in my eyes.

I peered over the person next to me to the view of Brazil, not that I could point anything out to you technically or with skill. Lush green peppered the landscape outside of the city, and my knees bounced with unconfined anticipation.

I just wanted to see her. Talk to her. Touch her perfect skin and look into her chocolate eyes and know that she was okay.

The rest of it didn't matter. Not what she wanted from me or didn't or the circumstances under which we'd parted ways.

Not the disapproval of the people around us or her reluctance to commit.

Not time or distance or some misspent effort to do what was right.

All that mattered was her.

All that ever mattered to me anymore was her.

Navigation through an airport and one cab ride later, and I had never been more thankful for the "Speak to Translate" app in my life.

I knew Portuguese was the language in Brazil, and I knew I

didn't speak it.

What I learned pretty quickly when I got there was that it was a problem.

I couldn't find an English speaker anywhere, and I didn't have time to seek one out. So instead, I spent what was probably five hundred million dollars and downloaded an app using international roaming data on my phone.

Luckily it had gotten me here, but under the duress of the situation, hours upon hours of travel, and the crushing relief of finally ending up in the building where Callie was, my memory did a good job of fleeing.

I rushed through the doors and to the front desk without one single look back to the cab, starting to speak as soon as I got within five feet.

"Callie Nickleson, please. Calia. You have to let me see her," I pleaded with the woman at the desk, waiting foolishly for her to answer me.

She shook her head in the negative, her understanding of even a single word I'd said failing.

I groaned to myself, grappling with my pockets and digging for my phone.

Before I could get it out though, a woman in scrubs approached the desk and looked at me appraisingly.

"Who are you here for?" she asked in perfect English, stopping the frantic search for my phone and freeing up a hand to squeeze the back of my tension-filled neck.

"Calia Nickleson."

"Are you family?" she asked, the dread that filled my stomach nearly sinking me to the floor when I realized that they weren't going to let me back there. Not only wasn't I family, but Callie was a public figure. There was no way they were going to just let any old schmo back there to see her.

"No, I'm …"

Looking over my face again, she interrupted me. "Are you Nik?"

My chin sank back into my chest.

"Yeah." Excitement made me stutter. "Yes."

She pursed her lips to the side. "Look, I'm sorry to be a pain, but I'm going to have to check your ID to make sure."

"Yeah, yeah," I agreed easily, "No problem." I reached quickly into my back pocket and pulled out the waiting passport.

She smiled warmly at the confirmation of my name, taking my elbow immediately and starting to walk.

"She's been waiting patiently for you."

My eyes teared up and very nearly spilled over. I wiped at the corners just in case.

"She's in surgery right now, but she made sure I knew to bring you back as soon as I could. *Keep checking to see if he gets here*, she told me over and over again before they took her back."

"Surgery?" I asked, forcing a swallow past my tight throat and scratching almost violently at the skin of my forehead. I felt positively itchy with anxiety and worry.

"On her back," she confirmed slowly.

Pulling me to a stop, she measured her words, cringing slightly as she lowered her voice.

"She was having some trouble feeling her legs."

Oh God.

I felt sick and uneasy on my feet and, given her reaction the evidence must have been splashed pretty clearly across my face.

Pushing me to the wall, she helped me settle my back against it and slide down, my butt hitting the floor and leaving room for my head between my knees.

She pushed actively on my neck, coaching me to keep my head down if I felt like I was going to pass out.

And I did.

I followed instruction and let the thoughts swirl endlessly like a bad loop of a nightmare on repeat.

I stewed and stewed, worrying every muscle so much they practically separated from the bone, knowing this kind of disability would break her.

She lived her life bottled inside herself most of the time, but her internal emotions were messy, fucked up, and relied heavily on the one thing she'd always held steady—her ability to release aggression and feeling through movement.

In that way, she really was like me.

"When you're ready we'll go to the waiting room. You can wait for her surgery to be over with her parents."

I hadn't thought it was possible before, but I quickly learned I could, in fact, be more nauseous.

I knew it was better to get it over with quickly though, so I pushed to my feet, swaying only slightly when ambushed by a wave of lightheadedness.

"She's gonna be fine, Nik," she comforted, naively thinking I only had one thing to worry about.

God, I didn't even know her name.

"What's your name?"

She smiled and patted my arm. "Shirley. And if you need anything you can ask for me."

I wanted to ask her more, like why she spoke English and anything and everything else I could think of about Callie. Her mental state and her spirits and how'd she'd been feeling besides the lack of feeling in her legs.

But before I could utter a word, we rounded the corner and came face to face with Frank and Sonya Nickleson.

His face warmed at the sight of Shirley but quickly turned to stone when he realized I was the one on her arm.

"What are you doing here?" he barked, surprising Shirley sig-

221

nificantly.

She was the only one.

My jaw hardened along with my resolve. The only way he was getting me out of here was by shooting me first. And even then, I'd make sure to request a room right fucking next door to his daughter.

"I'm here to see your daughter," I told him. My words were steel fact.

"Like hell—"

"Frank!" Callie's mom broke in, looking from my face to Frank's and back again.

"He's not going in there," he told her turning to look directly at her in order to issue the order.

"I'm sorry, sir, but I *am*," I corrected without waiting for his cold eyes to come back to me. "I already was, but now I've heard that Callie was asking for me herself. And if she wants to see me, you couldn't keep me away no matter how hard you tried."

My chest ached and heaved with each word as I fought to keep control of my volume. I wanted to yell and curse and punch him right in the nuts while I was at it, but the pesky rational voice in my head told me that wouldn't be a good idea or help *anyone* involved.

Scratch that.

It would help me. At least emotionally.

But not anyone else. Least of all, Callie.

And this was all about her.

His voice shifted to an angry whisper, the threat rolling easily off his tongue, "I'll have you physically removed—"

"Frank!" Sonya yelled loudly, startling us all.

My chin pulled back into my chest as I looked at this completely unknown version of Callie's mom with caution.

"Jesus, Frank, just stop. For Christ's sake, don't you think you've done about enough?"

As surprised as I was, Frank was mystified. It was astoundingly clear that Sonya Nickleson had never talked back to Frank a single day of their married lives. And maybe before.

But she was sure as hell talking back now.

"We're in goddamn Brazil, waiting on our daughter to come out of back surgery so we can find out if she's still got the use of her legs. Nik obviously traveled here as fast as he could, and Callie's asking for him, and by God, Frank, if she wants him, she's going to fucking get him."

The knot in my gut eased, the notion that I wasn't the only person here fighting to reunite me with Callie just barely lightening the burden.

I wasn't sure I trusted it enough to thank her verbally, but I met her eyes with my own and did my best to express my gratitude.

I looked from her to Frank and back again, and then watched as Shirley scooted quietly out of the room unnoticed. The other families looked on with interest, but no one said anything.

Not me, not Sonya, and most surprisingly, not Frank.

Shock painted his face as he backed over to a chair and sat down.

I kept a few chairs between us, but ultimately sat down on the same wall and waited.

Waited for news.

Waited for Frank to threaten to kick me out again.

But mostly, I waited to see my girl's chocolate brown—

★CHAPTER TWENTY-SEVEN★

Callie

Eyes.

They were the last thing I saw in my dreams and the first thing I saw when I woke up. Brilliant blue and surrounded by lush, dark eyebrows, lashes, and hair, they smiled at the corners, shimmering with a wetness beyond their normal pools of water.

I was groggy and confused, but I knew those eyes, and most of all, I knew who they belonged to.

"Nik?" I croaked, my throat scratchy and sore.

My focus zeroed in, and the fuzziness of his face started to clear.

"Right here, Cal," he whispered, leaning forward to kiss the very apple of my cheek.

"Are you really here?"

He laughed and smoothed the loose hair back off of my face.

"Pretty sure." His thumb moved from the corner of my mouth to my ear and back again. "Otherwise the ten hour flight was a really god awful dream."

I tried to smile, curving my lips up and holding them there as long as I could.

"Rest," he whispered, rubbing at the corners of my eyes until they fully closed. "You've been through a lot, my little Pea. And I swear on my life I'll be here when you wake up again."

"Good," I murmured just as I was drifting off to sleep. "Cause if you're not here, I'll kill you dead."

"Calia. *Caliaaa*. Come on, sweetie, wake up for me."

Warm fingers rubbed at the hair on my arm, pulling it from one side to the other and back again. It was easier to wake up this time, but I still felt way more fatigued than I was used to.

"Mmm," I mumbled, not quite knowing what I was saying or who I was talking to yet.

"Hi, Calia," a female nurse chirped, and with the blur of her face I couldn't tell if I recognized her or not yet. "I'm Shirley."

"Hi, Shirley," I responded, simply because it felt like what I was supposed to do. And then I had a flash of something from the first time I'd woken up.

"Nik?"

"Nope," I heard his voice call out from the other side of the room. "You killed him good and dead."

"Huh?" I groaned, shaking my head to try to help clear it.

He chuckled, coming into my line of sight and resting his hand on my leg. "I guess you don't remember what you told me before you fell asleep."

Slowly things started to come back to me in pieces, my routine and the fall, and a whole lot of hours spent wondering when I could see Nik again.

I hadn't known he would come, and I hadn't expected it.

But I had sure as hell hoped.

Then being wheeled into surgery on my back, an effort to try to restore feeling to the lower half of my body, which no matter the outcome meant the end of my ability to do gymnastics ever again.

And as if the wound needed a little more salt rubbed in, my fall cost our team the gold.

Three Olympics. Three Team Silver Medals.

I thought I'd feel unsatisfied by that. That is would really burn and grate that I made all this effort, all of these sacrifices, and still hadn't managed to do better than before.

But I didn't feel that way at all. I felt like three Silver Olympic medals was still really fucking good. And most of all, I felt like I got what I really wanted out of that work, sweat, and blood—a life changing reward that changed the meaning of my life and filled my life with even more guts and glory.

I wanted to feel like I had everything I'd always wanted. I wanted that feeling of fulfillment.

And I found it in Nik.

He was the everything I'd been looking for. It just took me a while to realize what everything looked like.

It wasn't until the fourth time his hand moved from my knee to ankle that I realized what the fact that I had noticed meant.

"Nik ... I ... I can feel your hand."

He looked down, startled, so lost in his thoughts and his concentration on my face that he didn't even realize what it meant either. He thought he was hurting me, jerking it back like retreating from an overly hot surface.

"No, no!" I shouted to stop him. "Put it back." I lowered my voice to a whisper. "Please, put it back." He did, looking right into my eyes and listening. "I think I can feel my legs."

His eyes widened just before closing in relief, his fingertips sinking noticeably into the muscle of my blanket-covered thigh. Sweet sensation drifted into the skin around them, and my throat clogged in relief.

"Oh, thank God," I heard my mom say from the side of the room I'd yet to survey. My dad stood next to her silently, probably for the first time in his life.

I'd told myself that everything would be okay no matter what the outcome with my legs. That as long as I figured out a way to get Nik in my life and keep him, the rest really didn't matter. I had to hold on to that positivity before surgery.

But I could not deny the sweet melody that hummed through my veins at the realization that I wouldn't have to live with that burden—and that Nik wouldn't have to either.

Lost in my own relief, I hadn't noticed that the room was uncomfortably silent.

When several seconds passed and my dad still said nothing, I scrunched my eyebrows together and looked from him to Nik, at a complete loss for what was going on.

"Nik?" I asked, knowing he would be the one to tell me the truth out of the bunch. Even if he didn't want to, he respected me enough to do it.

"Cal," he murmured sweetly with a short swipe of his arm, "it's fine."

It was fine?

What was goddamn fine?

What the hell was going on here?

"No, damnit. I don't know what's going on, but I do know that it is *not* fine," I disagreed, anger running the line of my body, raising me taller in bed, and making Shirley hide a smirk and turn her head. "Someone is going to tell me why it's weird, and they're going to do it right *now.*"

Still, no one spoke, and as a result, I officially started to *lose my*

227

shit.

I met each and every one's eyes individually, holding them in the depths of my most violent stare until they turned repentant.

"Someone is going to tell me why I'm lying here after one of the biggest scares of my *life*, telling you I can *feel my legs*, and you're all denying me a well-deserved goddamn celebration!"

Shirley, the saucy minx, raised her hand.

Nik couldn't contain his laugh at the harmlessly shit-stirring gesture, and my dad's eyes turned hard at the beautiful sound.

Mine narrowed for a fight, but before I even opened my mouth, my mom changed everything I thought I knew, turned my whole parental world upside down, and elbowed him directly and with force in the gut.

He made a small noise as the air left him, accusatory eyes turning toward my mom but not challenging.

"Okay," I shrieked! "Now I'm *really* interested."

Nik sighed and moved at once, coming to sit on the bed in the space by my hip. His hands moved to my face, love bleeding from every facet of his tender hold, and lifted my lips to his once, twice, and touching his lips to mine a third time before looking into my eyes and explaining to the best of his ability despite a clear preference not to.

"It's pretty simple, Cal, and if you really thought about it, I'm sure you could figure it out on your own." He paused only briefly, touching his lips to mine once more and drawing a grumble from my dad once more. My lips followed his as they left, each touch like a tiny stitch in the hole he'd torn open in my heart when he left.

He shrugged with a simplicity that matched his statement. "I'm here. Your dad doesn't want me to be."

I closed my eyes and slammed my head back into the pillow, turning in my father's direction and prying them slowly open. "Still, Dad? Really? Jesus."

"Come on, Frank," my mom prompted my dad, pulling him toward the door of the room and trying to contain the situation. "We'll give you some time alone," she added, addressing me directly. It was pretty clear he didn't want to go, but he did anyway.

Shirley winked and followed them out of the room, and Nik didn't watch any of it.

He was too busy watching me.

His forehead met mine with a soft thunk, and his eyes closed as it did.

"I missed you, Cal."

I reached up and cupped his cheek, whispering, "I missed you too."

His face felt warm in my hand, and the flush of his cheeks matched my own. "I know I didn't always make the best choices when it came to us, and I'm sorry for them all. For each hurt, each inconsistency, each time I made you feel less worthy and wanted than you are."

His lips touched mine softly.

"I want an us," I said desperately, feeling like my point wasn't clear enough and not wanting to leave even an ounce of question. "I want you and me, and I want it forever."

A small smile pulled at the very corners of his mouth, and his hands gingerly took mine, turning them over until the palms faced up.

Under the lights, the glitter and New Skin glistened, and the evidence of my jumbled up words shone indisputably.

"I know, my little Pea. I know you want it, and I know I'm going to give it to you. You, your dad, Shirley ..." He smiled. "None of you could get rid of me if you tried."

Relief surged and sizzled, and determined not to waste any more time or opportunities, I blurted out the one thing that was long past due.

"I love you," we said at once, completely robbing me of my victory dance, a right of passage to be awarded for taking my foot out of my mouth first.

Smiles melted both of our faces, and the already negligible space between us dwindled significantly.

He didn't let me dwell on it long though, crushing his lips to mine and re-marking my mouth as his. His tongue traveled all the territory, visiting all of the corners and the residents and leaving his taste with the majority of the sensitive buds of my tongue.

He felt like home and happiness and like a long awaited prize awarded solely by being a prize idiot.

I'd denied it too long, fought it too hard, and waited too long to make him my everything.

I didn't intend to make that mistake ever again.

His forehead rolled back and forth on mine as I shook my head, wanting to let it go, wanting to live in the moment and move forward, but not being able to.

"Why'd you go?" I breathed, the sound just barely audible over the bustling noise of the hospital around us.

His forehead left mine and his vision narrowed in question, but his hands reached out to hold both of mine. "What do you mean?"

"I mean," I started with a huff, the frustration I'd felt that day hitting me as if it were happening all over again. "Why did you leave? Why did you sign that stupid fucking paper? Why did you leave without *saying* anything? Why'd you give up and give in when you did nothing but swear that you wouldn't? I've got nearly a million fucking whys that have done a million fucking laps in my head."

He shook his head, slow at first and increasing in speed as it went, stopping only to accuse me of his own injustice.

"You signed that paper first," he insisted, squeezing at my hands with more and more pressure as he did. He wasn't only telling me. He was reaffirming the actuality to himself.

And he definitely saw it as a certainty.

My heart jumped in my chest, and I searched my memory for my exact account.

But I hadn't signed *anything*.

Not when he first brought me in the office, not when he showed me the paper from Nik, and not when I left to call him.

Nothing made sense, and I shook my head vehemently to say so.

"I didn't sign anything, Nik."

"Fuck!" he yelled, jumping back off the bed and startling my heart into a beat double the speed. He'd figured something out, but my brain was only moving at half of his speed.

I tried to sit up fast enough to follow him, tried to move as he moved away, fighting desperately to keep him close and touching.

"Nik—" I called as he turned, his walk a perfect display of anger and exploitation. The door slammed into the wall on his way out and my monitors started to go off in distress.

I tried to throw back the covers and climb from my bed, but though my legs had feeling, they were hardly fully functional, and the pain as a result of trying to force it was excruciating.

"Ahhhh," I moaned in pain, gritting my teeth against it just as Shirley came running into the room.

"Sit back," she told me, helping me settle back into the pillows and giving me a stern eye as she did.

I widened my own, nodding to the escalation outside. "You expect me not to try to figure out what's going on?"

She didn't answer. Instead, I heard Nik's voice going higher and higher until my father's joined in, each one of them scraping and challenging for dominance.

I panicked they'd get kicked out, but so far they hadn't.

Nik's eventually won the war, the sound of him asking, "What did you do?" ringing out so loudly the whole floor had to have heard it.

My palms turned clammy at the growing possibility of what I feared would be true.

"You owe us an explanation!" Nik's voice boomed, sending a sharp knife right through my heart.

Because I knew what had to be. I didn't know the details, but I knew the painfully heartbreaking gist.

My dad had set us both up like a couple of fools, and in a game where I had already lost, I just found out that I lost double.

Ushered by my mother and a lesser known, fuming version of Nik, my dad made his way back inside my room.

"Dad?" I asked simply, knowing he knew I was smart enough to put all of basic pieces of the situation together.

"I did it," he admitted immediately, Nik's jaw hardening to the point that I thought it might shatter in the background.

His eyes met mine.

I expected details and a reason, something greater than selfish priorities, but something far more disappointing is the only thing that came.

"I created a problem, and I fixed it."

Rote and steady and comical in its simplicity, his voice held no emotion. No hesitation, no apology, and not one fucking ounce of regret.

"Nik!" I yelled watching him jump toward my dad in one smooth move. It cost him a lot, I could see it in the stormy flash of his eyes, but he stopped at the sound of my voice.

"*God*, Dad, how could you?!" Bitterness burned the lining of my throat and bile met it in the middle on its way up. Betrayed wholly by one of my most trusted allies.

"I did what I had to do to keep you from ruining my career," he justified easily. Way too easily.

"And nearly ruined my life."

He rolled his eyes. "Don't be so dramatic. It's not like I intended to keep you apart forever—"

"No," I interrupted, a single tear finally escaping my eye and floating down the line of my cheek. "Just long enough to make sure I didn't mess up any of your carefully schemed plans."

"The worst part is that you still don't get it," Nik cut in, unable to hold back his own emotion anymore. "You don't get that life's about more than achievements. It's about understanding and love and a genuine fucking desire to make the people you supposedly care about happy."

"I know you're focused," he added before my dad could speak up. "But I also know you're not blind." His words were pointed and cutting. "You could not have missed that your daughter was happy … and that you were the one taking it away."

"Mom?" I asked, not wanting to know the answer.

She shook her head in despair. "I didn't know." Her eyes flashed to my father in disgusted disapproval. "Not until recently."

"I want you to go," I told my father, barely able to look at him, all of the years of his command-like-suggestions stacking up in the back of my mind. I'd never thought him to be calculating, but he was. He was from the beginning.

The one who had changed was me. I'd been a better puppet, an easier target, and an easily swayed vote.

Not anymore.

From naive to aware in the blink of one Olympic fall's eye.

He didn't realize what was happening, I could see it in his eyes, the denial of his consequences.

But I wasn't deciding if I trusted him anymore or not.

It was already—

★ CHAPTER TWENTY-EIGHT ★

Nik

Done.

Family ties are usually for life. But when the binding breaks, it's nearly impossible to put them back together again. Not without a whole hell of a lot of cooperation and glue.

After a thankfully short stint, therapy was finally over for Callie, and so was her relationship with her father.

Her back had healed beautifully, but her father's scars were still just as ugly as ever. There'd been no reconciliation and no apology, and, when it came to the two of them, absolutely nothing resembling a happily ever after.

The harsh reality was that some people never learned their lessons.

Parents died.

Trusted loved ones turned out to be neither trusted nor unconditionally loving.

For Callie's dad, their relationship came with strings. Big, thick, Olympic-sized ones.

Rationally, I couldn't wrap my mind around it. He'd had to have known that eventually it would end. That she'd grow too old to compete, too tired to perform, and too burned out to care.

I guess he just always expected it to end on his terms.

She felt the sting of his loss every day, but I made sure to contain the burn. Loving and supporting her own decisions and desires with the same fervor that I invested in my own.

Step by step, I carried her burden, but it didn't feel remotely like weight. Not when she did the same for me.

"Nik?" she called from the bathroom, the sound of it echoing and bouncing down the hall to my spot on the couch with uncertainty.

It was rare that I couldn't get a read on what she was feeling anymore, but all mixed up and stirred together, I had to admit that on this one, I had no clue.

"What's up, Cal?" I asked as I walked, not getting an answer.

I quickened my steps and deepened my frown, making up possibilities in my head and then taking them back just as fast.

Callie was different. More open to solutions and a fan of necessary change. She'd handled the upheaval of her injury surprisingly well, but there were moments when she didn't.

It was my job to be there when she had them.

"They're gone," she said simply, as soon as I turned the corner.

Her eyes weren't pained or sad necessarily. Just reflective.

My mind searched for what she could be talking about but ultimately came up empty.

"What's gone?"

Instead of answering with words, she settled for a simple nod of her head.

I glanced down, following her line of sight exactly and landing on the palms of her hands.

Healed and whole, no ugly rips marred the surface and years worth of calluses had softened and pinked slightly. They looked normal to the layperson, and it took me hardly any time at all to figure out that was the problem.

"I resented them and hid them my entire life, embarrassment in school and relationships and everything in between," she murmured, tracing the lines on her palms and following each individual branch of the print with precision.

Captivated, I followed along with her, pausing a beat at the places where each line came together.

"But they were my whole identity." She laughed. "Hell, you pointed it out. And now that they're gone, I don't know how to keep from missing them."

I shrugged and pulled her hand to my face, putting my lips to the pristine palm and giving it a gentle kiss.

"It's the key to everything, Cal. Instead of looking for what's missing, be happy with what you've got."

A smirk transformed her face from troubled to trouble-making in one quick shift and confirmed that the hands weren't the part of this conversation that mattered.

"But then I never would have ended up with you."

I shook my head, but she grabbed it by both cheeks, stopping the movement and pulling my mouth down to meet hers.

"You changed me, Nik. There I was, so sure I wanted everything to stay the same and you taught me better."

The journey hadn't been easy, but she was worth fighting for.

I took her mouth with mine, but she pulled back one last time.

"I'm happy with what I've got," she breathed, thinking the words that ran through my own mind on a constant loop.

She looked at her hand in mine, and then squeezed.

"You're a good teacher, you know?" she asked cheekily.

"Oh yeah?"

"Yeah," she nodded with a smile.

"I learned to love those battered hands, but I learned to love you better."

EPILOGUE

Callie

Every story follows an arc, but mine was unconventional.

In some twisted way, the conflict *was* the resolution.

More than half of my struggle had been inner-turmoil about whether I could really handle the idea of being done or not.

Now, I was.

Period.

Accepting that was what opened the door to change and love and the life I wouldn't trade for anything.

"How's it feel to be opening the doors to your own gym just one short year after breaking your back at your third Olympic games?"

I laughed somewhat awkwardly at the question, shrugging my shoulders minutely.

"It feels better than last year."

The reporter smiled and nodded, congratulating me silently on not being a complete robot of a human being.

"And it's not just my gym," I corrected, pulling a squirming Nik into the frame. "It's ours."

He was the whole reason I opened the damn thing in the first place.

Not because he wanted me to or asked me to or thought it would be a good idea for something we could do together.

I did it for purely selfish reasons.

I did it because I wanted to watch him tumble every night until he couldn't anymore.

I did it because I wanted to spend those hours alone together learning and leaning on each other.

I shook my head on a smile, the edges of it freezing as Nik's body lowered down to one knee beside me.

When his hand turned over to hold out the ring, the palm of it sparkled with glitter.

"What do you say, Cal? Wanna make a little extra magic with me?"

THE END

★ ACKNOWLEDGEMENTS ★

I'm extremely fortunate to have tons of supportive people in my life. But, as always, the first person I have to thank is my mom. She's the first person to have eyes on my book, even when it's in pieces, and is an invaluable source of encouragement and wisdom. And she's not a bad editor either. Lol! Thanks, Mamalicious!

My proofreaders! You guys were absolute champs. You help me put out the best product possible, and I really can't thank you enough for it!

My author friends. There are a ton of you, and you're all AWESOME. Thank you for sprinting with me, pushing me to keep writing, lifting me up, and assuring me that I really COULD do this.

M. Mabie, Aly Martinez, NA Alcorn. The set of you is trouble, but it's the kind I like to have.

Bx3 ladies. You guys are it. End. Of. Story. You lift me up when I'm down, make me laugh through it all, and support me unconditionally better than any group I've ever known.

Blogs. Um, hello, none of us could do this without you. I definitely couldn't do this without you. You all work so hard, and so many of you have supported me in ways that I can never thank you enough for. But I'll try. Thank you, thank you, thank you! I'd list you, but then

I'll forget someone and be devastated. Bad mojo.

You. The readers. Sweet baby Jesus, you guys are awesome. Every message, every comment—they mean everything to me. I spend hundreds of hours working on these books, and just one message from one of you—someone who saw something in my book, was touched in some special way—makes it worth it.

And, of course, I have to thank my family. My husband and son sacrifice the most, going without food and attention in order to let me push through to my deadline. Thank you for your support and for believing that this book is going to be something big.

ABOUT THE AUTHOR

Laurel Ulen Curtis is a 28 year old mother of one. She lives with her husband and son (and cat!) in New Jersey, but grew up all over the United States. She graduated from Rutgers University in 2009 with a Bachelor of Science in Meteorology, and puts that to almost no use other than forecasting for her friends and writing a storm chasing heroine! She has a passion for her family, laughing, and reading and writing Romance novels. She's also addicted to Coke. The drink, not the drug.

Laurel's Social Media:

Facebook: http://www.facebook.com/laurelulencurtis

Website: http://Laurelulencurtis.blogspot.com

Goodreads:
https://www.goodreads.com/author/show/6912103.Laurel_Ulen_Curtis

Instagram: https://instagram.com/lucurtisauthor/

Twitter: https://twitter.com/LUCurtisAuthor

Sign up for my Newsletter for news, giveaways, and more:
http://bit.ly/1JOfBuQ

Bloggers! Never miss a signup! Join my ALWAYS Blogger list:
http://bit.ly/1Kg8iuj

Other Books by Laurel:

The One Series:
The One Place
The One Girl

Impossible (Huntsford Hearts, #1)

The A is for Alpha Male Series
A is for Alpha Male
Secret Alpha
Accidental Alpha

One Last Night: A Novella

Hate: A Love Story

Quirks & Kinks

Coming Soon:
Ellie's Beat (A Hate Prequel Novel)
Untitled (A is for Alpha Male, #4)
Fated (Huntsford Hearts, #2)

Made in the USA
San Bernardino, CA
18 July 2018